D0036215

V I N T A G E

INTERNATIONAL

Oh What a
Paradise It Seems

John Cheever

Oh What a
Paradise It Seems

VINTAGE INTERNATIONAL · VINTAGE BOOKS
A Division of Random House, Inc. · New York

FIRST VINTAGE INTERNATIONAL EDITION,
OCTOBER 1991

Copyright © 1982 by John Cheever

All rights reserved under International and
Pan-American Copyright Conventions. Published in the
United States by Vintage Books, a division of
Random House, Inc., New York, and simultaneously in
Canada by Random House of Canada Limited, Toronto.
Originally published in hardcover by
Alfred A. Knopf, Inc., New York, in 1982.

Library of Congress Cataloging-in-Publication Data
Cheever, John.
Oh what a paradise it seems / John Cheever.—
1st Vintage International ed.
p. cm.
ISBN 0-679-73785-5 (pbk.)
I. Title.
PS3505.H6428O3 . 1991
813'.52—dc20   91-55305
CIP

Manufactured in the United States of America
10 9 8 7 6 5 4 3

To Benjamin Hale Cheever

Oh What a
Paradise It Seems

1

THIS is a story to be read in bed in an old house on a rainy night. The dogs are asleep and the saddle horses — Dombey and Trey — can be heard in their stalls across the dirt road beyond the orchard. The rain is gentle and needed but not needed with any desperation. The water tables are equitable, the nearby river is plentiful, the gardens and orchards — it is at a turning of the season — are irrigated ideally. Almost all the lights are out in the little village by the waterfall where the mill, so many years ago, used to produce gingham.

The granite walls of the mill still stand on the banks of the broad river and the mill owner's house with its four Corinthian columns still crowns the only hill in town. You might think of it as a sleepy village, out of touch with a changing world, but in the weekly newspaper Unidentified Flying Objects are reported with great frequency. They are reported not only by housewives hanging out their clothes and by sportsmen hunting squirrels, but they have been seen by substantial members of the population, such as the vice-president of the bank and the wife of the chief of police.

Walking through the village, from north to south, you were bound to notice the number of dogs and that they were all high-spirited and that they were without exception mongrels but mongrels with the marked characteristics of their mixed parentage and breeding. You might see a smooth-haired poodle, an Airedale with very short legs, or a dog that seemed to begin as a collie and ended as a Great Dane. These mixtures of blood—this newness of blood, you might say—had made them a highly spirited pack, and they hurried through the empty streets, late it seemed for some important meal, assignation or meeting, quite unfamiliar with the loneliness from which some of the population seemed to suffer. The town was named Janice after the mill owner's first wife.

One of the most extraordinary things about the village and its place in history was that it presented no fast-food franchises of any sort. This was very unusual at the time and would lead one to imagine that the village suffered from some sort of affliction, such as great poverty or a lack of adventure among its people; but it was simply an error on the part of those computers on whose authority the sites for fast-food franchises are chosen. Another historical peculiarity of the place was the fact that its large mansions, those relics of another time, had not been reconstructed to serve as nursing homes for that vast population of the comatose and the dying who were kept alive, unconscionably, through trailblazing medical invention.

At the north end of the town was Beasley's Pond—a deep body of water, shaped like a bent arm, with heavily forested shores. Here were water and greenery, and if one were a nineteenth-century painter one would put into the foreground a lovely woman on a mule, bent a little over the child she held and accompanied by a man with a staff. This would enable the artist to label the painting "Flight into Egypt," although all he had meant to commemorate was his bewildering pleasure in a fine landscape on a summer's day.

An aged man is but a paltry thing, a tattered coat upon a stick, unless he sees the bright plumage of the bird called courage—*Cardinalis virginius,* in this case—and oh how his heart leapt. But what was a cardinal bird doing on East 78th Street? He called his oldest daughter, who lived in Janice, and asked if there was any skating. Their friendship was a highly practical relationship, characterized principally by skepticism. She said that it had been very cold, there was no snow, and while she had seen no skaters on the big pond she guessed that it was frozen. His skates, she knew, were in the attic along with his Piranesi folio and his collection of mounted butterflies. This was on a Sunday morning in late January and he took a train, a local, to the province where his daughter lived.

His name was Lemuel Sears. He was, as I say, an old man but not yet infirm. One would not have to help him across the street. He was old enough to remember when the horizons of his country were dominated by the beautiful and lachrymose wine-glass elm tree and when most of the bathtubs one stepped into had lions' claws. He was old enough to remember the promise of dirigible travel, and he would never forget marching into one of the capital cities of the Holy Roman Empire. Turn and turn-about bombing had left nothing standing of this great crossroads that was higher than a man's shoulder. In the ruined cathedral lay the unburied dead. It was a lovely summer's day. He was armed with the earliest of the gas-recoil rifles (M-1), prepared to kill the enemy and defend with his life the freedoms of speech, religion and travel.

His daughter kissed him lightly. Their relationship was, as I say, skeptical but quite profound. She was the daughter of sainted Amelia, his first wife. She handed him his skates and offered to drive him to the pond but he chose to walk. It was around four miles and he wore a business suit with a vest and a fur hat bought in one of the Eastern European countries where he had frequently traveled on business for a computer-container manufacturer. He had white hair that grew like quack grass and a cat-boat tan. He was of that generation and class that regard overcoats as a desperate last measure. Of course he wore gloves. The pond he walked to was called Beasley's Pond but no one seemed to remember who the Beasleys had been. The pond was two and one half or three miles if one took the distance from end to end. It seemed to be frozen, although there were only four or five skaters on the ice and this was a clement Sunday afternoon.

Glancing at the scene Sears thought of how the eighteenth- and nineteenth-century Dutch painters had cornered the skating scene and that before the values of the art market had become chaotic there were usually, at the end of the art auction, half a dozen unsold Dutch skating scenes leaning against the unsold umbrella stand beside the unwanted harpsichord. Brueghel had done some skating scenes but Sears had seen a skating scene—a drawing—from a much earlier period—the twelfth century he thought—and he always happily remembered Alan Gardener, the English paleontologist whose career was built on the thesis that the skate—or shate, since this came before any known language—had given *Homo sapiens,* as a hunter, the velocity that enabled him to outstrip Neanderthal man in the contest for supremacy. This was two hundred thousand years ago, much of the earth was covered with ice and the shate was made of the skull of the Judsas broadbill. That Alan Gardener's thesis was all a fabrication was revealed very late in his career, but Sears found the poetry of his ideas abiding because the fleetness he felt on skates seemed to have the depth of an ancient experience, and he had always been partial to any attempt to defraud the academic universe.

He put on his skates and moved off. This was quite as natural to him as swimming. He wondered why there were so few skaters on the ice and he asked a young woman. She was barely marriageable, with dark hair and gold rings in her ears, and she carried a hockey stick like a parasol. "I know, I know," she said, "but you see it hasn't been frozen over like this for over a century. It's been more than a century since it's been this cold without snow. Isn't it heavenly? I love it, I like it, I like it, I love it." He had heard exactly that exclamation from a lover so many years ago that he could not remember her name or the color of her hair or precisely what the erotic acrobatics were that they were performing.

He skated and skated. The pleasure of fleetness seemed, as she had said, divine. Swinging down a long stretch of black ice gave Sears a sense of homecoming. At long last, at the end of a cold, long journey, he was returning to a place where his name was known and loved and lamps burned in the rooms and fires in the hearth. It seemed to Sears that all the skaters moved over the ice with the happy conviction that they were on their way home. Home might be an empty room and an empty bed to many of them, including Sears, but swinging over the black ice convinced Sears that he was on his way home. Someone more skeptical might point out that this illuminated how ephemeral is our illusion of homecoming. There was a winter sunset and in this formidable show of light and color he unlaced his skates and returned to his apartment in the city.

But next Sunday he was back on the ice and this time there were more people. There were perhaps fifty—a small number for such a vast expanse of ice. A hockey rink had been improvised and somewhere to the left of this was an area where most of the skaters seemed to be accomplished at cutting figures; but most of the population, like Sears, simply went up and down, up and down, completely absorbed in the illusion that fleetness and grace were in their possession and had only to be revealed. Sears fell once or twice but then so did almost everyone else. Toward the end of the afternoon he maneuvered an accomplished brake-turn and stopped to listen to the voices of the skaters.

It was late. The shadow of a hill had darkened half the ice. The hockey game was in its last moments and the figure skaters had taken off their gear and gone home. The voices, considering the imminence of night, had an extraordinary lightness that reminded him of voices from a Mediterranean beach before, through the savagery of pollution, that coast was lost to us. He and his companions on the ice seemed to enjoy that extraordinary preoccupation with innocence that absorbs people on a beach before the fall of darkness. So he skated again until the sunset, kissed his skeptical but loving daughter goodbye and returned to his place in the city.

It was two weeks or more later when Sears returned with his skates to find that the ice had melted and Beasley's Pond was being used for a dump. It was a blow. Nearly a third of it had already been despoiled and on his right he saw the shell of a ten-year-old automobile and a little closer to him a dead dog. He thought his heart would break.

Why celebrate a dump, why endeavor to describe an aberration? Here was the discharge of a society that was inclined to nomadism without having lessened its passion for portables. Most wandering people evolve a culture of tents and saddles and migratory herds, but here was a wandering people with a passion for gigantic bedsteads and massive refrigerators. It was a clash between their mobility—their driftingness—and their love of permanence that had discharged its chaos into Beasley's Pond.

Why dwell on a disaster—and it was an absolute disaster that Sears saw, but a disaster with a power of melancholy. Most men have bought for their beloved an electric toaster or a vacuum cleaner and have been rewarded with transports of bliss. To see these souvenirs of our early loves spread-eagled, rusted and upended by the force with which they were cast off can be a profoundly melancholy experience. Thousands upon thousands of wire clothes hangers sounded the only homely and genuine note.

When he returned to the city Sears called his law firm and asked them to investigate the tragedy of Beasley's Pond. He also wrote a letter to the newspaper.

2

T HE revolutionary discovery of the cerbical chip with its memory capacity infinitely greater than the silicon chip's had necessitated Sears's making several trips to the cerbical mines in the Carpathians and to the new deposits that had been discovered in the Danube Valley. At the time of which I'm writing both the silicon RAM and the ROM contained fewer than 16,000 facts, and while the silicon 64K contained 65,536 bits of information, the new VLSI circuit, introduced by the cerbical chip, contained more than a million pieces of information. A study completed by Thompson-Howard tended to support the superiority of cerbical chips. TH had tested 300,000 chips and found the cerbical freer of defects. The fact that the firm Sears worked for manufactured intrusion systems for computer containers kept him continuously exposed to the computer memory with its supernatural command of facts and its supernatural lack of discernment, and this may have heightened his concern with sentimental matters such as the end of his skating and the destruction of Beasley's Pond. Quite recently yet another sentimental encounter had become his concern.

The time of which I'm writing was a time in our history when the line or queue had been seriously challenged by automation, particularly in banks. Customers were urged by newspaper advertisements, television and mailings to make their deposits and withdrawals by inserting cards into responsive machines, but there were still enough men and women who had mislaid their cards or who were so lonely that they liked to smile at a teller to form a friendly line at a bank window. They were of that generation who imagined there to be a line at the gates of heaven. Some force of change could be felt in the lines, but it was no more than the change one might notice in an airport a day or so after the fare to Rome or San Francisco had been increased. The air was filled with faint and random music.

She was two or three ahead of him—a remarkably good-looking woman who was an inch or so shorter than he although she wore high heels. She was small enough to be held—a consideration that he had come to think of as practical. Her figure was splendid and endearing. He thought that perhaps it was nostalgia that made her countenance such a forceful experience for him. It could have been that he was growing old and feared the end of love. The possibility of such a loss was much on his mind. When in the movies he saw a man and a woman kiss ardently he would wonder if this was a country which tomorrow or the day after he would be expected to leave. When he saw a couple in the street embrace with deep tenderness or walk delightedly shoulder to shoulder, he would be reminded, for no more than a moment, of his approaching age. This could have contributed to the fact that he thought her presence stunning. Her looks aroused the most forthright and robust memories: the flag being raised at the ballpark before the first pitch while a baritone sang the National Anthem. This was an exaggeration; but the memories her appearance summoned involved only brightness. Her hair was a modest yellow. Her eyes, when she took off her large dark glasses, would, he knew, be violet. In her rather small features he saw nothing at all like a mountain range and yet here was very definitely a declaration of paradise, either mountainous or maritime, depending upon one's tastes. He might have been regarding some great beach on another day of the week, but today he seemed to see the mountains, seemed disposed to raise his eyes, his head, and brace his shoulders as we do when, driving along some ghastly gambling-house strip, we see snow-covered mountains and feel how enduring is their challenge and their beauty. The components of his life seemed to present the need for a bridge and she and he seemed competent to build one that morning in the bank. She would, as a girl and a young woman, have been thought very pretty and this was an element—a grain—in the presence. She could have been the winsome girl on the oleomargarine package or the Oriental dancer on his father's cigar box who used to stir his little prick when he was about nine.

The music that filled the air of the bank at that hour was a Brandenburg Concerto, played as ragtime. He imagined the smoothness of her naked back—its marked absence of declivity—so like a promised land. He wanted her as a lover, of course, and he felt that a profound and gratifying erotic consummation is a glimpse at another's immortal soul as one's own immortal soul is shown. Our lovers are always as tall as or taller than we. He stepped out of line, tapped her lightly on the shoulder and said: "I wonder if

you can tell me what the music is that they're playing. You
look to me as if you understood music."

"You don't understand the first thing about women,"
she said. She laughed sweetly and dropped some papers
she carried. Most of these he saw, when he picked them up,
were real-estate advertisements, and when he passed them
back to her he asked if she was in the real-estate business.
She said yes and he said he was looking for an apartment.
She gave him a card with the name Renée Herndon and
they returned to their places in line.

Sears was quite content with his apartment on East
78th Street. He was not a dishonest man and when he
telephoned Renée Herndon a few days later he fully intended
to reward her generously for any time she spent with him.
He said he was looking for a one- or two-room apartment,
and that he was prepared to pay a substantial rent and sign
at least a two-year lease. She agreed to show him what was
available the next afternoon.

The offices where she worked struck him as being characterized by a kind of netherness. They were on the nether
floor of a nether building in a nether neighborhood, and
when he entered the place he saw nothing that was not
distinguished by its portability. The reception room deco-
rated with a vast urn, filled with artificial grasses and
weeds, the receptionist's desk, the receptionist herself all
seemed highly mobile as if they could be moved, at short
notice, to another building, another state or even another
country. Renée Herndon, when she joined him, seemed

quite permanent. Her hold on his attention, his senses and his intelligence was quite the most he knew of permanence, at that point in his life.

She was, he guessed, thirty-five or perhaps forty and would have been married once or maybe twice. Her past was, at this point, none of his business. She was the sunny side of the street. The uniformity with which women of her age then dressed—widowed or divorced, showing real estate or working in china shops—seemed nearly ordained. She wore a suit, a little good perfume and no hat. He would have liked to kiss her, as she well knew, and when they got to the street and he offered her his arm she took it warmly and smiled or laughed with pleasure. She said they could either walk or take a cab and he said that he would be delighted to walk.

They had walked for no more than half a block when she was attracted—magnetized was the word—to a display of embroidered scarves in a window. Still holding his arm she admired these. He offered to buy her one of the scarves and she politely refused, but her refusal was, he thought from his experience, genuine. He had known many women whose refusals were transparent. He felt that her distinct refusal to let a stranger buy her a present displayed a glimpse at the proportions of her self-respect. He thought this intimate and lovely. He was also delighted to see that in the three blocks they had to walk from her office to the apartment she was to show him she stopped to look at the display in absolutely every window with the exception of a window that displayed surgical appliances. They looked at shoes and hats and dresses and pottery animals and jewelry and china, and her interest in everything there was for sale charmed him and seemed to promise that she shared with him an undisciplined enthusiasm for men and women and circumstances and changes in the weather. The apartment she showed him was very different.

At about this time the high incidence of criminal rapes and robberies made it difficult to get into apartments in some neighborhoods, and though she had keys and credentials they had great difficulties with a doorman, whose uniform was unbuttoned and who cleaned his teeth, while he talked to them, with an old-fashioned kitchen match. When they finally got inside, the uniformity of the dim lights in the corridors, the sameness of the doors and the great difficulty she had in finding the place seemed to expose him to the loneliness of penance. The apartment that she showed him was a sort of nomadic hideout—it was still furnished with the chairs and tables of a divorcee whose lover or gigolo had abandoned her, although she still had photographs of him—many of them naked—hung on her bedroom wall. There was a narrow terrace from which you could see some blue sky, but the broad light of day could never reach the apartment.

She knew, of course, that he would not want it and said so. "I don't," she said, "know why I ever showed it to you. I detest the place myself." "It's given me an opportunity to ask you to dinner," he said. "I'd love to have dinner with you," she said, "if you don't mind having a late dinner. I'm busy early in the evening." "The time," he said, "makes no difference."

They walked back, now on the other side of the street,

looking at the gloves, shoes, antiques, embroideries and paintings that were displayed. "When do we meet?" he asked when they reached the door to her office. "Thursday?" she asked. "Meet me in the parish house of St. Anselm's at about nine-fifteen on Thursday." Then she was gone.

St. Anselm's was Presbyterian and he wondered what she could be doing there on a weekday night. This was in Lent and the only church observations would be mournful. He didn't know but he thought the Presbyterians had a less exacting calendar than his own Episcopal Church, and he guessed that Thursday was not a church holiday and that she had not gone to church to pray. None of his wives or lovers had been enthusiastic church members and this might be the first time in his life that he had gone to church to meet a woman. St. Anselm's was on Park Avenue in a good neighborhood—that is a neighborhood where wealth was of the first importance. The main entrance to the church was dark and locked, but the parish-house door around the corner was lighted and unlocked. He let himself into a large vestibule. There was a second door—royal in its proportions. A sign was thumbtacked to this: MEMBERS ONLY. THIS IS A CLOSED MEETING. The sign was amateurish and he could imagine some woman—neither young nor beautiful but charmingly earnest—working on the sign at a kitchen table. Sears's imagination was inclined to be optimistic and that the gathering beyond the closed doors involved membership— some vow or commitment or oath— did not seem to him sinister. He thought perhaps that dues were paid. He did not feel that to take a look at the gathering would in any way involve an intrusion and he opened the door a crack.

He saw an ecclesiastical meeting room or auditorium — one of those places where the rummage sale would be held and the nativity play would be performed. He looked into the faces of forty men and women who were listening attentively to a speaker at a podium. He was at once struck by his incompetence at judging the gathering. Not even in times of war, with which he was familiar, not even in the evacuation of burning cities had he seen so mixed a gathering. It was a group, he thought, in which there was nowhere the force of selection. Since the faces — young, old, haggard and serene — conveyed nothing to him, he looked at their clothing and found even fewer bearings. They wore the clothes of the rich, the clothes of the poor and a few cheap imitations of the rich. Who were they: who in the world could they be? Here were the plain, cheerful faces of the mixed nationalities that distinguished his country.

He looked at the woman on the podium. She was a black-haired woman, perhaps in her forties, wearing one of those long nondescript dresses known as evening dresses although they are worn to weddings, christenings and barbecues. She was reading a list of names. Three men and two women came to the platform as she called their names. One of the women was bent with age, surely a septuagenarian. One of the men was perhaps nineteen. He had three cowlicks and a high color and wore a sweatshirt with Odium University printed on it. Beside him was a blond young man in a full suit and next was his beloved Renée, wearing one of those very simple frocks that cost a little less than a good used car. She looked as lovely—as bright—as she had looked to him from the start.

"Turn out the lights, Charlie," said the woman in the long dress. The lights went out and after a minute or two of suspense a door opened and a man came in carrying one of those flat, cheap cakes with candles that are ordered to celebrate the retirement of the building maintenance assistant or the oldest member of the stenographic pool. The lights went on and the gathering got to their feet and sang in the customary genuinely sincere and tuneless voices, "Happy anniversary to you, Happy anniversary, dear celebrant . . ." Renée smiled, laughed, and seemed truly happy with their wishes, and he looked back at the congregation. It seemed that he should be able to make some sense of the variety in their faces, and then he found himself, countenance by countenance, man and woman, young and old, trying to imagine how their faces would look contorted by the throes of erotic love. He was chagrined at his willingness to invade their lives—he was ashamed of himself and he closed the door.

A workman was sweeping the vestibule. "What is going on in there?" Sears asked. "I don't know," the workman said. "They're either trying to stop smoking or drinking or eating but I don't remember which bunch is in there tonight. It's the no smokers that give me a pain in the ass. I smoke a pack, maybe a pack and a half a day, I sweep up cigarette butts, that's my job, that's what I get paid for and it's nobody's business but my own. For instance I went to pay my state tax last week. This is in a government building, this is in a building I pay for and right on the wall there is this sign that says THANK YOU FOR NOT SMOKING. How the hell do they know that I'm not going to smoke? How do they know that I'm not going to piss or fart or get a hard-on? Thank you for not smoking. What the hell business is it of theirs? Thank you for not breathing. . . . " Then he went out a door.

A few minutes later Sears heard the group recite something in unison. He guessed from the eagerness and clarity in their voices that it could not be an occult mantra. It was difficult to imagine what it could be. The cadence had for Sears the familiarity of church scripture and might have been the Lord's Prayer or the Twenty-third Psalm, but there was some sameness to the cadence in the seventeenth-century translations of scripture and unless he was told he would never know what they were chanting.

Then the doors opened and they came out — not like a crowd discharged at the end of an entertainment or a lecture but gradually, like the crowd at the close of a social gathering, and he had, after all, seen them blow the candles out on a cake. He looked for her, he sought her brightness as he had for all his long life looked for lovely women in airports and railroad stations and ships' piers and now in a parish house. He saw her, as bright as ever, and he went to her and she took his arm as they went out the door and he hailed a cab on the avenue. "What in the world were you doing in there?" he asked, when they were in the cab. "Will you promise not to ask me that again?" she said. "I know this must sound unreasonable — I would think it unreasonable if I were you — but I spend quite a few nights in parish houses and I'd just as soon not tell anyone why. If you ever take me out on Friday you'll have to pick me up at the New School for Social Research. If you want to know what I'm doing there I'll tell you."

"What are you doing at the New School for Social Research?"

"I'm taking a course in accounting."

"Is this for business?"

"No. It's to help me understand my income tax."

"That's clever."

"You don't," she laughed, "understand the first thing about women."

He had booked a table at the most expensive restaurant where he was known. To his surprise, she was just as well known as he. The headwaiter greeted him warmly but he greeted her just as warmly. That she was intelligently aware of her attractiveness was apparent to Sears as he walked behind her to their table and saw how she carried herself. It was knowledgeable—so much so that he saw one waiter wink to another. This only increased the fun so far as he was concerned. For a first course he ordered some cold trout, most of which she ate. He ordered a '73 Montrachet but he noticed that she hardly drank her wine. She tasted his soup and said it was too salty but when he was served his duck *printanier* she ate as much of it as he did. She also enjoyed her own meal. Sears seldom ate sweets but she ate a *crème brûlée* while she told him what she pleased about herself.

She was divorced from a successful dentist named Arthur and had two children. Her son, who was eighteen, was absorbed in Eastern religions, but from what she said

Sears wasn't sure whether or not he was in Tibet. Her daughter was in a ballet school in Des Moines, where Arthur lived. She said without sarcasm or laughter that she was at a turning point in her affairs. He felt that the time had not yet come for him to tell her that he was not really looking for an apartment although, considering the gait of her conversation, she might already know. "I hope we can go back to your place after dinner," he said. "My place is such a wreck that I would be ashamed to show it to you."

"But that's why I'm here," she said with a brightness that threatened to depress him for a moment but seemed then only a fair maneuver on her part. "I'm going to show you a new apartment. There is supposed to be a place in the eighties with two bedrooms and a marvelous view of the bridges. I thought we could see it after dinner."

He paid for the dinner with a credit card and when she saw the amount of the tip he wrote on the receipt she said, softly and sadly: "That's too much, that's really too much."

They took a cab to the apartment that was for rent. There was no difficulty with the doorman but the building seemed to Sears vast and labyrinthine. Forty or fifty stories in the air she unlocked the door on a tiny room that had a view of the river and its bridges and their lights. This was charming but distant. There were a very small bedroom and a kitchen and a locked door. She tried several keys in the door. "I know there's another bedroom with a view of the city," she said. "It says so here." She showed him some duplicated piece of paper that described two bedrooms, one spacious with a view of the city. But the door was locked. None of the keys she had would unlock it. She tried them all and so did Sears. "It doesn't really matter," he said. "I don't want to see the other bedroom. The living room is really too small. I mean I couldn't get any of my furniture into it. Don't worry about showing me the other room."

Worry was it; she was worried. When the keys wouldn't open the door she tried to force the lock with her hand. She kicked the door. Sears then remembered a scene with Estelle, his second wife. It was in some airport—London, he guessed. They had taken a night flight and it was three-thirty by their watches—an unholy hour. They were exhausted and deeply disoriented, and because of some strike or slowdown or some increase in passengers because of some historical catastrophe or celebration—an earthquake or a coronation— the whole process of claiming one's luggage and having its contents checked for contraband was unconscionably delayed. Before they were cleared there was dawn over London—a despairing light on this particular morning. He cleared the bags and was carrying them to the queue for cabs when Estelle stopped and tried to open a door on which NO ADMITTANCE was written in every known European language as well as in the Cyrillic alphabet. She tried to force the door's hardware as Renée had done. She pounded on the EINTRITT IST VERBOTEN sign with her fists and then, as Renée was doing now, she began to cry, to sob.

He felt then for his wife how much he loved her and how absolutely ignorant he was of the commandment that ruled her life. She seemed, pounding on the door in the London dawn, to have come from a creation about which he knew nothing although they had slept in each other's arms for years. His feeling for Renée was confused and profound and when she began to cry he took her in his arms, not to solace her for the locked door of course but to comfort her for Arthur and every other disappointment in her life. She wept on his shoulder for a little while and then they locked up the apartment and took a cab downtown. He kissed her in the cab and her lips were as soft as anything he had ever known and he thought that he would never forget their softness; and he never did. She wore a little more perfume than she wore in business hours, and he loved the smell, but when he touched her breasts she gently took his hand away and said: "Not tonight, darling, some other time." She lived in the fifties and he kissed her goodbye in front of her apartment and asked when he could see her again. "I'll be at the 83rd Street Baptist Church on Monday night," she said. "Sometime between nine-fifteen and nine-thirty. You can't ever tell when the meeting will end."

On the next day Sears received a letter from a junior member of his law firm — a man he had not met — announcing the death, the murder, of the lawyer Sears had asked to investigate the pollution of Beasley's Pond. The lawyer had ascertained, before his murder, that the Janice Planning Board had rezoned the pond for "fill" and given the property a tax-exempt status as a future war memorial. If Sears wanted to pursue the matter the young lawyer recommended an environmentalist named Horace Chisholm.

3

I wish this story I'm telling began with the fragrance of mint growing along a stream bed where I'm lying, concealed with my rifle, waiting to assassinate a pretender who is expected to come here, fishing for trout. What I can see of the sky is blue. The smell of mint is very strong and I hear the music of water. The pretender is a well-favored young man and thinks himself quite alone. There is, he seems to think, some blessedness in fishing trout with flies. He sings while he assembles his rod and looks up at the sky and around at the trees to reassure himself of the naturalness of this garden from which, unknown to him, he is about to be dismissed. My rifle is loaded and I put it to my shoulder and take the location of his heart in my cross-sights. The smell of mint seriously challenges the rightness of this or any other murder. . . . Yes, I would much sooner be occupied with such matters than with the death of the Salazzos' old dog Buster, but at the time of which I'm writing the purity of the water was of inexorable interest—far more important than dynasties—and the Salazzos are linked to the purity of Beasley's Pond.

Sammy Salazzo ran one of the three barbershops in the village. He was a good man and a good barber but he never seemed to make ends meet. He lived in one of those little houses in Hitching Post Lane, a neighborhood that was once mentioned on Metropolitan television when it was swept by a plague of measles. The occupancy of a house there was signified by the fact that some sort of brazier for cooking meat over coals stood in the backyard. When the brazier went it meant that the family had gone and the house was for sale. The architecture was all happy ending— all greeting card—that is, it seemed to have been evolved by a people who were exiles or refugees and who thought obsessively of returning. The variety of these homesteads was international. They were English Tudor, they were Spanish, they were nostalgic for the recent past or the efficient simplicities of some future, but they all expressed, very powerfully, a sense of endings and returns. Anything about these houses that seemed artificial or vulgar was justified by the fact that they were meant to represent a serene retirement.

It had been a bad day at the tag end of winter. No one had come near the barbershop excepting the mailman and he had only delivered bills. Sam closed up the place at five and went home, coasting down the hills in his car to save gasoline. It is with the most genuine reluctance that I describe the house he returned to and the asininity of the game show that his wife and two daughters were watching on television. It was a show where a wheel was spun and when the winner was given merchandise, travel tickets and sometimes cash the award-giving was very noisy and demonstrative. Buster, the old dog, greeted him. "Where's my supper?" Sammy asked. He had to shout to be heard over the television.

"There isn't any supper," his wife said, "there's nothing to eat in the house but dog food."

"I give you money to buy food," shouted Sammy. "What do you do with it? Throw it in the street?"

"With the money you give me I can't buy nothing but dog food," shouted his wife.

"Well, if we ain't going to eat, Buster ain't going to eat," shouted Sammy. "If I have to shoot Buster to get that through your dumb head that's what I'm going to do." His wife and his daughters either didn't believe him or were too absorbed in their television show to pay any attention to his announcement.

He got his rifle together and loaded the weapon. Then he went into the living room and turned off the TV. "You're all going to see this," he said. "It's about time somebody around here realized how serious life is. We can't go on welfare because I got this business but we got to make sacrifices and Buster is going to be the first sacrifice we make."

Both of the children began to cry, "Oh no, no, Daddy, no, no." In years to come, both of his daughters, lying naked in the arms of strangers, would say with as much intimacy as a declaration of love: "Did I ever tell you about the night Daddy shot the dog?" But now they were children, bewildered by the adult world and by a scene that would bewilder anyone in its grotesqueness. We know very little about the canine intelligence and nothing at all about the canine sense of eternity, but Buster seemed to understand what was expected of him and to welcome the chance to play a useful role in the life of the family even if it cost him his own life. The children were screaming. Maria's sobbing was profound and life appeared to her a chaos with no guiding lights of any sort. Sammy led the old dog out into the backyard and asked him to sit down a little to the right of the charcoal brazier. He then backed away a few yards and shot him through the heart.

As soon as she saw this, Maria went to the telephone and called Sam's Uncle Luigi and said she had to see him. Sam came from one of those south of Naples families whose bonds had been strengthened by their emigration to a new world. Luigi ran the family restaurant out on the old post-road spur that fed into the four-digit interstate. She didn't ask to see Luigi, she simply told him that she was on her way.

Luigi's was one of those Italian restaurants that remind us all of how truly new is our settlement on this continent and how many of us here are still strangers. The rudiments of southern Italy—its archways and masonry—were here, but like some plant that has been transported thoughtlessly to alien soil the archways seemed to have lost some of their ancient usefulness and beauty and taken on new attributes. The place had passed from one branch of the family to another and had changed its name and its specialties again and again. It had been Emilio's and Giovanni's; it had had topless dancers and black singers and at one time it had even advertised Chinese cooking. When Maria came into the place that night a stranger in a dirty tuxedo asked her what she wanted and when she said that she wanted to see Luigi he said Luigi was unavailable. She pushed past him and opened a door beyond the bar, where she found Luigi watching a news show on television.

"Oh Lou, Lou," she said, and she was crying. "I know I'm not Italian and none of you think I can cook and most of the family treat me like a stranger but now you've got to try and help. Like about twenty minutes ago he took the dog out in the backyard and shot him where everybody could see. It's just that we don't have any money. We don't need very much. We don't need much at all. He doesn't have nobody but the family. He won't even join the volunteer fire department. I'm too old to work in fast-food places and I can't sew fast enough for that sweatshop in Lansville. You've got to help us."

"Sam's not sick?"

"No, he's not sick, he's not even sick in the head, he's just worried sick that's all."

"You live near the pond she's a called Beasley's?" Luigi asked.

"Yes. We live on Hitching Post Lane. It's about half a mile away."

"You tell him he comes here tomorrow afternoon."

The chain of energy in the Salazzo organization was exactingly familial and traditional. Their home in southern Italy had been along the sea before the Mediterranean had been bankrupted but they had none of the attributes of a maritime people with the exception of pirates. Nor were they like a mountain people. Perhaps all one could say was that they were a people who had been very poor. The exalted members of the family asked the governor to their weddings and two of them had had dinner in the White House. Sam knew this rank of the Salazzos mostly from what he read in the papers. He was one of a large number of barbers, gas pumpers and masons who made up the Salazzo proletariat. All of this was true until the night he shot the dog. The next night a large black car stopped by the house and a young man — not a member of the family — invited Sam to be vice-chairman of the governor's committee for the impartial uses of Beasley's Pond. He would be paid a salary three times what he made on a good day in the barbershop. He was to avoid any sort of show — he was not, for example, to buy a new car — but the organization would help him to profitably invest his savings. His only duties were to collect cash payment for the dumping of fill in Beasley's Pond.

Three days later Sam put a FOR RENT sign in the barbershop window and at seven one morning went out to Beasley's Pond where a five-axle, eighteen-wheel dump truck was waiting. The rate was eighty dollars a load and on his first day Sam took in close to six thousand dollars. He kept a ledger to record the dumping and had been given a leather bag for the cash. He knew enough to be scrupulously honest, and while the reputation of southern Italians as murderers was highly exaggerated, he had no disposition to steal. Each night at seven with some punctuality, two men in a large black car stopped at his house to collect the cash.

The collectors were not particularly sinister. The older of them was one of those small, old Italians who always wear their hats tipped forward over their brows as if they were, even in the rain, enduring the glare of an equinoctial sun. These same old men walk with their knees quite high in the air as if they were forever climbing those hills on the summits of which so much of Italy stands. The younger man had a mustache and smiled a great deal. They both refused wine and coffee—they refused to sit down—and on Fridays they paid Sam his salary. It was a great deal more money than he had ever had before and he parceled this out to Maria although he was not ungenerous.

The only other witness to the assassination of Buster had been Betsy Logan, who lived in the house next to the Salazzos. She was a young woman with two small children whose husband worked in the post office. The Salazzos and the Logans were not friendly neighbors, perhaps because the Salazzos' daughters were too old to play with Betsy Logan's sons. The only closeness had been with Buster, who came over to the Logans for table scraps; and when Betsy saw Sam murder the old dog she felt nothing for her neighbor but hatred and contempt. She noticed the FOR RENT sign in the barbershop window and saw from her kitchen window the strangers who came to the house each night at dusk. From the rubbish that was dumped into the pond Sam had salvaged a broken overstuffed chair and he sat in this while he collected his fees. Betsy had seen Sam reposing in this as she drove out toward Buy Brite on the interstate. He seemed to be supervising the death of Beasley's Pond, although Betsy would always think of him as the murderer of an old and friendly dog.

4

I N the next month or so Sears became familiar with a
great many parish houses and church basements as well
as with the vicinity of the New School for Social Research,
where she studied accounting on Friday nights. He was
constitutionally a traditional specimen with a traditional
and at times benighted concept of a woman's role in the
world, but her unchallengeable good looks seemed, so far
as he was concerned, to secure her place in the stream of
things. A good-looking woman studying arithmetic seemed
to him something of a lark, and the people in her class in
accounting presented an earnest, friendly and readily accept-
able appearance. However, the other gatherings where she
sometimes spent three nights a week continued to disturb
him with their violent lack of uniformity. Night after night
they looked like the crowd scattered by a thunderstorm on the
evening of some holiday in any park in the Western world.

The janitor had told him that these gatherings aimed at
abstinence in sex, food, alcohol and tobacco. He had suffered
a good deal of embarrassment from carnal importunacy
but he could not imagine tempering this in a drafty parish
house. He had never smoked, his weight was constant and
he thoroughly enjoyed drinking. As I say, the authority of
her good looks—she seemed too friendly to be thought a

beauty—made her association with this weird crowd some-what palatable. She let him kiss her goodnight and he would, for the softness of her lips and the fragrance of her breasts, have waited for her in a condemned mine shaft. She was, as women go, relatively punctual and Sears had come to believe that punctuality in engagements was an infallible gauge of sexual spontaneity. He had observed that, without exception, women who were tardy for dinner engagements were unconsciously delayed in their erotic transports and that women who were early for lunch or dinner would sometimes climax in the taxi on their way home.

Renée had nothing to do, of course, with the length of these sessions that she attended and Sears knew nothing but pleasure in waiting for her in parish houses and church basements, and watching the crowd with whom she chose to associate had begun to interest him, partly because they were her associates, partly because he was obliged by circumstances to regard them and because they so discon-certingly challenged his common sense. The traditional forces of selection—the clubs, the social register and the professional lists—were all obsolete, he knew, but some traces or hints of caste seemed necessary to him for the comprehension and enjoyment of the world. These people seemed not only to belong to no organized society, they seemed to confound any such possibility. They were a genuine cross-section—something he abhorred.

But since abstinence, continence, some intangible moral value was at the bottom of this group, how could he have expected anything but a disparate gathering? The life of the spirit had no part, it seemed, in the establishment of caste.

Not, at least, in the Western World. Early Christianity cut the widest swath. So, coming from a generation that could, perhaps, be characterized by the vastness of its disposition to complain, he didn't suppose that he could scorn men and women who must be looking for something better. That things had been better was the music, the reprise of his days. It had been sung by his elders, by his associates, he had heard it sung in college by Toynbee and Spengler. Things had been better, things were getting worse, and the lengthening moral and intellectual shadows that one saw spreading over the Western World were final. What a bore it had been to live in this self-induced autumnal twilight! He supposed that these strangers—this queer congregation— would agree with him. However, he would not dream of abdicating his airs and pretenses for their company.

But she was always there—lightness and swiftness and the sense of an agility that flatteringly complemented his age. They dined and joked and she kissed him goodnight in the street by her house until one evening when she telephoned him and invited him to meet her, not in some church basement but in her apartment. "Don't bother to make a reservation," she said. "I'll cook the dinner here."

That was a rainy night. It would be very unlike Sears to ally the sound of rain to his limited knowledge of love but there was, in fact, some alliance. It seemed that the most he knew of love had been revealed to him while he heard the music of rain. Light showers, heavy rains, torrential rains, floods, in fact, seemed joined in his memory to loving although this did not cross his mind while he bathed, very carefully, and dressed that evening. The importance of rain is agricultural and plenty may have been involved, since plenteousness is one aspect of love. Darkness to some degree belongs to rain and darkness to some degree belongs to love. In countless beds he had numbered his blessings while he heard the rain on the roof, heard it drip from a faulty gutter, heard it fall into fields and gardens and on the roofs and backyards of many cities. He walked across the city that night in the rain.

At the time of which I'm writing jogging was very popular in every city of the world with which he was familiar. Toward the end of the day in Rotterdam or Moscow, in the brilliant winter afterglow that New York sometimes enjoys or in the early snows in Copenhagen you would find men and women of every imaginable age and specification going forth to enjoy a run. The only rewards for these exertions were small and worthless trophies. Commercialization would come, of course, but it would come later, and jogging was then one of the few taxing human endeavors that had absolutely nothing to do with the banks. One evening in Amsterdam or Leningrad—Sears couldn't remember the city but he must have known something of the language— Sears had stopped a dozen joggers and asked them why they ran. "I run to find myself," they said, "I run to lose weight, I run because I'm in love, I run to forget my debts, I run because I've had a stiff prick for the last three weeks and I hope to cool it, I run to escape my mother-in-law, I run for the glory of God." He found all the answers gratifying and understandable, and now whenever at dusk in Bucharest or Des Moines, in Venice or Calgary he saw the runners appear they seemed to him the salt of the earth, they seemed to him stubborn and irreducible proof of man's determination to excel. As he crossed the city that rainy night he was passed by many runners.

She met him at the door wearing a wrapper, a shabby blue wrapper. He was out of his clothes in a minute. "You were hardpacked," she said sweetly, sometime later. "You've burned the vegetables," he said. "I put everything on the back of the stove when you telephoned from the lobby," said she. He spent the night and left at around nine. Elevator men, janitors, the whole service population play an important role of approval or shock in our extracurricular appearances, and the elevator man in Renée's apartment seemed surprised and bewildered by Sears's appearance. His look of bewilderment was followed by a look of solicitude as if Sears aroused in him some concern. He asked if he could get Sears a taxi. Sears thanked him and said no. Sears thought him already a member of the cast and wondered how the tip for Christmas was arranged in that particular building, although it was not yet Easter.

Oh the wind and the rain! Back in Janice Maria Salazzo bought some wind chimes at Buy Brite when she had some extra money after Sam shot the dog.

Betsy first heard the chimes one night in early spring when she was getting supper. Sam had hung them from the ceiling of the Salazzos' back porch, which was very close to the Logans' kitchen, and even when Betsy closed the window she could hear the music of the wind chimes. That night their music woke her. It was three in the morning and she couldn't get back to sleep. The wind chimes seemed to speak to her although she wanted nothing to do with them.

She blamed herself. She disliked the Salazzos because they had killed their dog and she disliked everything else about them including their wind chimes. It was her fault that she couldn't get back to sleep until dawn and when the alarm woke her the next thing she heard was the music of the wind chimes.

Betsy was working part time as a file clerk at the Scandinavian Lamp Factory, but when she came home from work and paid off the old lady who sat with Binxie she heard the wind chimes again. She closed the window. She still seemed to hear them and she went upstairs and closed all the windows on that side of the house. It was a warm evening for that time of year and when Henry came home and kissed her he asked why all the windows were shut. "The Salazzos' wind chimes are driving me crazy," Betsy said. "I may be neurotic or something but I hate the noise they make." "I'll turn up the TV so you can't hear it," said Henry, and he did, but when he turned off the TV and they went to bed at about eleven she could hear the wind chimes again, telling their dumb, continuous story in a language she could not understand. She imagined the Salazzos to be much less sensitive and refined than she and Henry and she guessed that their insensitivity involved an indifference to the sounds of the world around them, including the sounds of their wind chimes. However, they woke her again at three and kept her pretty much awake until dawn. She could not discern what she found so troubling in the noise they made but she thought they made a troublesome noise. When she came home the next night and was taking off her shoes she called her friend Liz Holland and told her about the problem.

"Well, ask her to take them down," Liz said. "Just tell her they're driving you crazy. Or maybe first ask her politely if she can hear them and if the noise doesn't bother her. Why don't you try that?"

At that time of year the Salazzos almost never came out of their house except to go to work. It was too cold for them to have filled their new stand-up swimming pool and there wasn't any grass to cut. Betsy didn't want to bring up the problem on the telephone but the next night when she was unwrapping some frozen vegetables she saw Maria Salazzo come down the back stairs with a garbage container. Betsy ran out of the house and crossed the yard. "Hasn't it been a nice day?" she asked.

"It depends on what you were doing," said Maria. She banged the garbage container against the pail. Betsy had been told that she sometimes drank a lot. She hoped she wasn't drunk. "I see you have new wind chimes," said Betsy.

"I got them at a sale at Buy Brite," said Maria, "but I think they're all gone. I got a friend in the Oriental Arts business who might be able to get you a set."

"Oh, I don't want any," Betsy said. "I just wondered if you can hear them as loudly as we can."

"Of course I can hear them," Maria said. "What do you think I bought them for?"

"Well, the thing is we can hear them too much," said Betsy. She was struggling. To say that they kept her awake would seem to state that she was an enfeebled sleeper. "I mean I wondered if you couldn't turn them off at night."

"You must be going crazy," said Maria. "You think I can turn off the wind?"

5

DURING the weeks that followed Renée refused to take any presents from Sears. She gave him a scarf, gloves and a pair of cuff links but when he gave her a piece of jewelry she made him return it. "You don't," she said, kissing him, "understand the first thing about women." Sears's sexual demands had given him a great deal of pleasure, some embarrassment and a painful suspicion that the polarities in his constitution were acutely incompatible and that the only myth that suited his disposition was Dr. Jekyll and Mr. Hyde. He'd never read the book but he had seen the movie. Renée's understanding, her willingness to accommodate him in taxis and hallways was of a beauty that he could not remember ever having experienced before. There was an unspoken understanding between them. She had once said, over her shoulder, that male discharges were, in her experience the most restorative face cream and while he had heard this remark he had swiftly forgotten it since the clinical aspects of carnality were not what he sought. His importunacy and her deep concern with youthfulness were facts but facts that he would dismiss since in constructing a useful paradigm for love there are various organic needs that seem to contribute nothing to the pleasure we take in one another. They both had something the other wanted.

She was, in his long experience, the kind of woman whose front hall was always a mess. She was the kind of woman who always forgot to buy oranges and when you woke with her in your arms you would realize that the first thing you had to do was to put on your pants and go out and buy fruit. She was the kind of woman who, as soon as she entered her apartment, turned on first the lights and then the record player. Music had been playing when he first entered her apartment and it would be playing when he was long gone and forgotten. He knew from experience that silence—the absence of music—was for some men and women as suspect as darkness. It seemed a genuine need like protein or sugar but in his case continuous music presented a problem he had never before encountered. One night when they were making love the record player was performing a romantic piano concerto that closed with a long chain of percussive, false and volcanic climaxes. Every time the pianist seemed about to ascend his final peak he would fall away from the summit into a whole spectrum of lower octaves and start his ascent once more, as would Sears. Finally Renée asked, with great tenderness: "Aren't you ever going to come?" "Not until the pianist does," said Sears. This was quite true and they concluded their performances simultaneously. He never knew whether or not she had understood him.

He would have described her as a clever woman although from time to time she surprised and disappointed him. She knew absolutely nothing about radioactivity. When he came in one evening, very tired from a board meeting, and tried to explain what had tired him, she seemed bored and uncomprehending although he thought it simple enough. The conglomerate that owned his firm had, that afternoon, acquired an airline whose sales were three times as large as theirs. No conglomerate, he explained, should be overly committed. As she well knew, specialization of any sort could be very dangerous. Consider nuclear investedness: The cost of mining uranium had gone from ten to nearly forty dollars a pound while the price had dropped from forty dollars a pound to just under twenty-eight. The airline they'd bought only needed dynamic top executives to reverse their last year's losses of twenty million. When she whistled at this news she completely failed to understand that the superiority of his firm lay in the fact that they had lost thirty-seven million. However, he would have described her as a clever woman.

Her sister came to town and he was not to see Renée for a week or so. He missed her keenly. The physical deprivation was considerable and acute. On the day that her sister left she agreed to meet him for lunch and invited him to her place at one. He imagined that she would greet him in her old blue wrapper and that after they had made love he would send out for sandwiches. Dressing for the rendezvous he tried to remember what ties, shirts and suits she had said she liked, but then it occurred to him that he would be out of his clothes a minute or two after he entered her apartment and that there was no point in deliberating over his wardrobe. He even decided against underwear lest it delay his achieving nakedness. As we watch Sears put his genitals into his trousers it is worth observing the look on his face.

Sears was a thoughtful man and there was no effrontery or arrogance here, but he seemed to enjoy something very like authority, as if this most commonplace organ, possessed by absolutely every other man on the planet, were some singular treasure, such as the pen that was used for signing the Treaty of Versailles, robbing Bulgaria of Macedonia, giving her Aegean coast to Greece, creating several new quarrelsome nations in the Balkans, expatriating and leaving homeless large populations, giving Poland a corridor to the Baltic and sowing the seeds for future discord and war. Putting his genitals into his trousers Sears seemed to think he was handling history.

There were no cabs that day. He more or less ran to her apartment and was winded when he got into the elevator in her building. "Twelve B," he said to the elevator operator. It was the same man who had taken him down on his first morning. His face seemed to Sears to possess some innocence and so he could not attribute meanness to the exchange that followed.

"Are you her father?" the elevator man asked.

"No," said Sears. He could barely speak.

"Her grandfather?"

"I am her uncle," said Sears.

"Then you must have known her when she was a little girl," said the elevator man. "She must have been terribly pretty. She's beautiful now but I keep thinking about how she must have looked when she was a girl."

It was a blow to Sears, a stunning blow, although he should have been able to anticipate this in the way she wagged her ass around. Just following her to a table in a restaurant inaugurated an erotic competition that would leave the waiters, and any other players, obliged to dismiss Sears as an old man who, with his clothes off, would present nothing interesting but a costly wristwatch. He had been aware of the competition but he had always thought himself victorious. The blow was devastating.

When she opened the door she was not wearing her old blue wrapper. She was wearing the suit she had been wearing when she first showed him an apartment, and she also wore gloves and a hat. She was wearing the glasses she wore to read by and another pair of glasses—dark— either for cosmetic reasons or to screen the light.

"Oh, my darling," he groaned.

"I've made a reservation at the Tombeau de Couperin," she said.

"I've missed you terribly," he said. "I'm so hardpacked that I can't eat." He unbuckled his trousers and let them fall to his knees.

"I'm sorry," she said, "but I cannot help you."

"Don't you speak to me like that," he said. "Don't talk to me as if you were a department-store clerk talking to some customer about a discontinued line. You know perfectly well that you can help me."

"There is nothing between us," she said.

"I've fucked you a hundred times," he shouted, "and if that's nothing I think you highly immoral. I've hoped all morning to see you in your blue wrapper and you've got everything on but the slip covers."

"Are you or are you not going to take me to lunch?" she

said. "If you're too distracted I have a standing invitation from plenty of other men."

"I'll get some flowers," he said. He pulled up and fastened his trousers. "Wait here. I'll be right back."

She truly loved cut flowers, he thought. Cut flowers had for her a seductive force, and with cut flowers that sternness, so unlike her, would surely yield. He ran to the florist nearest her apartment but the place was closed. He hailed a cab and asked to be taken to a florist. It was a long search but they found one, where he bought two dozen yellow roses. Yellow was her color. He had often heard her say that she loved yellow. Back at her apartment he rang her bell for quite some time—a half hour, perhaps—before he would acknowledge the fact that she had gone out.

Now there are, it seemed to Sears, some Balkans of the spirit, where the villages are lit by fire and the bears weigh upwards of seven hundred pounds, and to which he now found himself quite helplessly being transported. Sears had taken many business trips to the Balkans and he was truly familiar with this world. He imagined some Monday morning—some Blue Monday—at the turn of the year, November probably, when snow was expected and his hotel room was cold. There was no hot water for shaving, there was no water of any sort and no way of procuring any. He dressed and went out to find that the elevator wasn't working. He walked down five or six flights of malodorous and shabby stairs to the café. The only person there was a homely waitress in a very dirty uniform who was wiping the dust off a rubber plant with a page of an untruthful newspaper the tyrannical government published for propaganda purposes, distorting all the facts including the weather and the rainfall. When he asked for coffee— that most international word—the waitress made an ugly face and he realized that he was in one of those provinces that had suffered the Turkish Occupation for centuries and that had seen no coffee since its liberation by Alexander the Second in 1878.

He went out onto the street. The street was named to commemorate the Plebescite of April the Third. He turned right, looking for coffee, onto Eleanor Markova Street. He didn't know it but Eleanor Markova had, at some time in the forties, been martyred by the Fascists. Markova Street led to Liberation Street and he followed this to Freedom Avenue, Proletariat Boulevard and Victory Square. He smelled coffee nowhere and saw no smiles, no beauty of any sort, no brow even that promised comprehension as brows will.

Sears had been raised by open-hearted and loving men and women, and why such a forlorn mountain city should have established itself in his consciousness was mysterious. He was truly a stranger to hostility of any sort and yet, at the moment, hostility seemed to be his home. He had loved his dear parents, he had loved and been loved by his teachers and friends, love had illuminated even his military experience, and so why then should he seem so susceptible to a hostility that he had never known?

He seemed to have reached his Balkans by plane. The plane was large and he traveled first class, but he found himself in some airport where no one could tell him when his plane would depart and no one anyhow could speak any language that he knew. His grief was more the grief of a traveler than a lover. The grueling search for his baggage, the ridiculous attempt to charm the customs police, the wish to send to college those venereal vagrants who haunt airport urinals had all contributed to his sense of abandonment and his gathering fear.

The elevator door opened. It was not she. It was the elevator operator. He was wearing street clothes and a hat. He went directly to where Sears stood and embraced him. Sears put his head against the man's shoulder. The stranger's embrace seemed to comprehend that newfound province of loneliness that had frightened Sears. He seemed to know all about that mountainous city where there was no beauty and no coffee and where a homely waitress wiped a rubber plant's leaves with an untruthful newspaper. What the elevator man then said came as a great surprise to Sears. "I've worried about you ever since that first morning," he said. What he then did came as an even greater surprise to Sears. Sears had tried genuinely to bring to his venereal drives something like the rectitude of Burke's *Peerage,* the New York Social Register or the early days of the Metropolitan Club. These congregations were, he knew, not truly selective but they had the radiance, the shine, of something chosen, an air of ordination that he unthinkingly admired. The stranger, whose name he hadn't learned, took him downstairs to a small room off the lobby, where he undressed Sears and undressed himself. Sears's next stop, of course, was a psychiatrist.

6

O NE of the several pleasures of Betsy's life was visiting
Buy Brite, a massive store in the shopping mall on the
four-digit interstate. She liked — she loved — to push a cart
with nice rubber-tired wheels through a paradise of groceries,
vegetables, meats, fishes, breads and cakes to the music
she danced to the year she fell in love with Henry. Then
when she paid for what she had chosen she would be given
a number that might name her the winner of one hundred
thousand dollars or a trip to someplace like Honolulu.
Betsy was not at all interested in the paleontological history of barter and marketing, but the purity and simplicity
of the bounty she saw at Buy Brite were like a reminder of
the markets and festivals of our earlier history.

It is because our fortresses were meant to be impregnable
that the fortresses of the ancient world have outlasted the
marketplaces of the past, leaving the impression that fear
and bellicosity were the keystones of our earliest communi-
ties, when in fact those crossroads where men met to barter
fish for baskets, greens for meat and gold for brides were
the places where we first grew to know and communicate
with one another. Some part of Betsy's excitement at Buy
Brite may have been due to the fact that she was participat-
ing in one of the earliest rites of our civilization.

She had gone to Buy Brite that afternoon, leaving the children alone at home, in order to buy a bottle of soap that she had found efficient, sympathetic and cheap. This was called Flotilla. At Buy Brite there was a single entrance and exit. The corridor for soaps was a great distance from the entrance, and on her way there Betsy picked up a bag of potatoes (marked down), a jar of Teriyaki Sauce, a box of crackers, a dozen eggs and a pair of Argyle socks. She was careful to keep her purchases under ten so that she could use the express lane. Randy was an intelligent and obedient child but emergencies could always arise. There was the afternoon when he had gotten drunk on vanilla extract and been found playing with matches.

Now Betsy would have noticed the music that played while she looked for Flotilla only, perhaps, if it had been music that she had danced to or music that reminded her of the pleasures of dancing. Betsy was of that generation for whom the air was, oftener than not, filled with music. She heard music everywhere; she sometimes heard music on the telephone while she waited for her call to be completed. In some ways this had left her imperceptive. She would never have noticed that morning that the air of Buy Brite was filled with some of the greatest music of the eighteenth century.

This music had been chosen by a nephew of one of the majority stockholders, who seemed to think that there would be some enjoyable irony between eighteenth-century music and the tumult of a contemporary shopping center. He was, spiritually speaking, a frail young man who would amount to nothing, and the irony he so enjoyed would be discontinued and forgotten in a month or so. There is no irony, of course. The capital of Brandenburg was a market village and on a summer's day when the doors of the cathedral stood open the great concertos must have been heard by the grocers and merchants. Betsy pushed her cart toward the express lane to the music that has contributed more, perhaps, than any other voice to our concept of nobility. Betsy pushed her cart toward lane 9—the express lane.

Maria Salazzo was also there. Having, for as long as she could remember, examined the price of everything she bought, and tried not very successfully to cut their expenses by collecting coupons, to go to the store with a hundred dollars or more to spend was for her a new experience, a sense of freedom and power that was quite heady. It was because of this exciting sense of power perhaps that she headed for the express lane, in spite of the fact that her cart was heaped with groceries. She headed for the lane at the same time as Betsy. The scene with the wind chimes had left some enmity between them and they did not speak. They were neck and neck but Maria, moved perhaps by her sense of wealth, passed Betsy on her right. The queue was fairly long because at that time of day—twilight—shoppers were picking up what they had forgotten for dinner. First was a young man with two cans of cat food. Next was a black man with a bag of potato chips, a box of cheese, a can of apple juice and a novel about sex life in Las Vegas. After him was a woman with a dozen oranges in a bag, followed by Maria with a week's groceries. The clerk was too tired to send her away and began to check her groceries through on the register.

Betsy saw through the window that a light rain had

begun to fall. She was worried about having left the children alone. Maybelle was the name of the checkout clerk and she wore a large pin that said so. "Maybelle," said Betsy, "would you kindly explain to this lady that this lane is the express lane for shoppers with nine items only."

"If she can't read I'm not going to teach her," said Maybelle. The twelve or so members in the line behind Betsy showed their approval. "It's about time somebody said something," said a black.

"You tell 'em, lady, you tell 'em," said an old man with a frozen dinner. "I just can't stand to see someone take advantage of other people's kindness. It's like fascism. It isn't that she's breaking the law. It's just that most of us are too nice to do anything about it. Why do you suppose they put up a sign that says nine items? It's to make the store more efficient for everyone. You're just like a shoplifter only you're not stealing groceries, you're stealing time, you're not stealing from the management, you're stealing from us. People like you cause wars."

"Will you shut up," said Maria. "Will you mind your own business!"

"It happens to be our business," said Betsy. "It's everybody's business. That sign up there says it's for nine items or less and it's for anybody who can read."

"They don't care," said Maria.

"What did they put the sign up for if they don't care?"

"Well, I know one thing," said Maria. "They didn't put the sign up so that troublemakers like you could interfere in other people's business."

"It is everybody's business," said Betsy. "It's just like

driving on the right-hand side of the road. There are a few basic rules or the business of life comes to a standstill. I've left my two children at home alone because I counted on being able to check through the express lane without waiting for someone with a week's groceries."

"You tell her, lady, you tell her," called a man way back in the line. "You've got my vote."

"This line is for nine items or less," said Betsy, "and I'm going to see that we stick to the rule." She picked a dozen eggs off the counter and put them back into Maria's cart. Maria grabbed her hand and the eggs fell to the floor and broke.

"You keep your hands off my groceries," shouted Maria. "You keep your hands off my groceries or I'll call the police." She reached into Betsy's cart, took out a dozen eggs and threw them onto the floor.

Then Betsy, in an overwhelming paroxysm of anger, seized Maria's cart and, drawing it toward her, tipped all of the groceries onto the floor. Maria, quite as overwhelmed, and passionate as if she felt herself to be a figure in some ancient patriotic or religious contest, came at Betsy, swinging. Their raised voices, the screaming, drew a crowd, and perhaps a hundred shoppers, with their carts, gathered to watch these women fighting over groceries and precedents. The manager, helped by some members of the crowd, finally succeeded in parting the two women and sending them out on separate ways into the rainy dusk.

than he had ever felt on an overcast Monday morning in
some mountain village in the Carpathians. His doctor had
given him a list of psychiatrists and he chose a doctor
named Palmer because he had known a happy family of
that name in the elm-tree-shaded lanes of his serene coming of age. Dr. Palmer answered the telephone himself and
Sears made an appointment.

The doctor's office suffered that netherness that Sears
had observed in Renée's office. He shared a waiting room,
a toilet and some old magazines with a number of other
practitioners. He was a tall man whom Sears would have
described as ill-favored. Dr. Palmer was quite bald and the
impression that he gave was mostly of bulk. He seemed to
Sears mysteriously shabby, considering his East Side address,
but Sears would blame this on his own parochialism. He
was mistaken. Dr. Palmer was shabby because he was
desperately in need of money. He was quite unsuccessful,
plagued by the intensely internecine politics of his profession and worried about paying the rent. Considering the
area in which Sears sought counsel, his choice of Dr. Palmer
had been unlucky. Dr. Palmer was a homosexual spinster.

By "spinster" one means that Dr. Palmer, by a combina-
tion of ardent desire and pitiless repression, had exacer-
bated his feeling on the subject. He had, it seemed, from
time to time endured random erections for a naked and
anonymous male torso or the declivity of a male spine, and
he had treated these arousals with vigilant repression.
Indeed, he had crushed these random swellings as if they
breached that paradigm that furnished his equilibrium. He
was the victim of an erotic distress that in earlier and more

7

A T the time of which I'm writing, vogues in healing were changing swiftly, and many of the old-line of yesterday's therapists were wiping windshields in carwashes. While the nomenclature "shrink" was long out of fashion and had been replaced by the old term "psychoanalyst," the conviction that one could master the mysteriousness of life through the interpretation of dreams and an exhaustive analysis of one's early life was perhaps the most prevalent form of belief in the Western World. This stood, of course, four-square upon the ruins of the legitimate confessional and the reformation of the roles played by parents in one's coming of age. The Freudian vocabulary had sunk well into the vulgate, and when the waitress at a truck drivers' diner spilled your beer she would say: "Oops. That was a Freudian slip." If you asked her what she meant she would say: "What's the matter with you? Born yesterday? Freudian means slippery. Get with it."

Sears, seeking counsel, thought of the word "alienist" because it had been in use when he was a young man and because it described that anguish that had racked him when he stood with his roses by the unanswered door. There had been nothing, absolutely nothing unfamiliar in the scene and yet he had felt himself more cruelly estranged traditional societies had characterized the unmarried woman who played out a role that was marked by bitterness, suspicion and loneliness.

While Sears told the doctor about the day he had bought the yellow roses for Renée and what he and the elevator operator had done the doctor squirmed in his chair. "You seem to think it neurotic of me," said Sears politely, "to be anxious about being homosexual, but in retrospect it seems to me probably the most sensible anxiety I have ever entertained. I've never really had any reason to be anxious about money or friends or position or health, but I did enjoy myself with the elevator man and if I should have to declare myself a homosexual it would be the end of my life.

"My sexual nature seems to contain some self-destructive elements and I've come to you to have these explained. There seem to be contrary polarities in my constitution. I think my sexual conduct moral only in that it reflects on my concept of love. This seems to be of the first importance. Renée had hanging, in one of her windows, a small crystal cut with many facets. When this filled with light it threw a spectrum on the wall, and one late afternoon I said to her, quite sincerely, that my love for her was quite as important, as iridescent and as insubstantial, as the beam of colored light. She said that I didn't understand the first thing about women but she always said that. She once took my cock out of her mouth only long enough to tell me that I didn't understand the first thing about women."

The doctor's offices were on the fourth floor of an old-fashioned building with windows that opened and shut, and through these windows Sears then heard the loud, cheerful voice of a man calling some other man to throw him a ball. It was a voice from the playing field but the depth of his longing and nostalgia was not only for his youth but for the robustness, simplicity and beauty that life could possess; and how far he had strayed from this! He was paying the doctor's rent in a sincere attempt to recapture this simplicity and usefulness, but the distance he had come seemed grievous.

"What are you thinking about?" asked Dr. Palmer.

"I heard a voice from the street," said Sears. "It reminded me of summer days and happier times."

"Infantilism is obviously one of your greatest handicaps," said the doctor.

"I mean," said Sears, "that it reminded me of a fourth down with something like twenty to go. All you can do is to punt but how marvelous it is to punt, that feeling of booting a ball way down the field on a fourth down is such a hopeful feeling, such a feeling of beginning that I've often wondered why football never caught on in other countries."

"Did you ever make the first team?" asked Palmer.

"No, no," said Sears, quite sadly. "I was always second squad and a substitute some of the time."

"You're getting a little heavy," said the doctor.

Sears stood and said, "I'm wearing the belt I wore when I played football."

"Did you ever think of marrying?" asked the doctor.

"I was married twice," said Sears.

"Divorced?" asked the doctor.

"Both of my wives died," said Sears.

"Hmmmm," said Dr. Palmer.

Sears had met his first wife—beloved Amelia—at the intermission of a concert in Boston. Her hair was that light-brown hue that, early in life, turns a lovely yellow during a long summer spent sensibly on beaches, boat decks and tennis courts. This crowning with yellow passes swiftly—that may be one of its charms—and the gift is lost in one's early twenties. Their encounter came late in October; she was barely twenty and her hair was streaked with gold. This contrasted with her eyebrows. These were uncommonly heavy and dark and she carried her head in a lifted manner as if her eyebrows were something of a burden. Her figure was superb and she wore that afternoon a black velvet dress and carried a copy of *Paris Match*, folded to a page where there was a recipe for codfish served with cheese sauce. Sears felt at once that he had known her in some other life and he would never have any occasion to question the authority of this sensation of familiarity. When she lay dying in his arms, twenty years later, his grief was unassuageable but there was a sense that she was returning to some stratum of existence where they had first met and where they would meet again.

His second wife was not so much his choice as he was hers. She had ended an unhappy, childless marriage with a divorce, and when she proposed to Sears he simply accepted. She claimed to have great insights into the future, and she assured Sears that they would be very happy together. After their marriage Sears discovered that Estelle, his wife, considered herself a professional in occult matters. She defended her prescience competitively as if supernatural insights were a field sport. Sears's only other experience in this area had been in Eastern Europe, where there was a celebrated prophetess named Gallia. Sears had heard of her mostly from American businessmen who traveled to the cave where she lived and paid large sums of money for her advice.

One evening, in Eastern Europe, a chance American drinking companion had described Gallia's powers to Sears. She had prophesied an accident at their New Mexico mines, where millions of gallons of radioactive mill tailings would have been spilled. She had also, that year, prophesied that uranium prices would fall. Sears had been told that she had been blinded by lightning as a child and that she lived in an extinct volcano, not far from where one of the most famous oracles of the ancient world had lived. The Minister of Information had often offered to try and arrange a meeting with Gallia, but Sears's lack of interest in the occult was genuine. Returning one late afternoon to his hotel after a tiring day, he found an aide to the Minister of Information in the lobby with the message that Gallia would see him. He asked if there was time to change his shirt and he was told there was not. He got into one of those large cars that cabinet ministers enjoy in socialist countries.

In the car he joined his interpreter, a middle-aged woman whose language with him would be French. The minister had furnished the car with some ice and a bottle of whiskey. Sears was terribly tired. The car radio was on, very loud, and Sears knew enough not to have it turned off; it would be such a disappointment to the chauffeur. There is some sameness to car radio music all over the world and he would hear Hoagy Carmichael's "Stardust" and the second Razumovsky Quartet. In that part of the world there were regular reports on the water level of the Danube River. It was a country where there were very few cars, and they traveled through the farmland at a hundred miles an hour. This splendid rich country was farmed still by hand. He was not that afternoon to see a single piece of farm machinery, and although it was late in the day men and women were still hoeing the rows. A few of these waved happily to the limousine. The beauty of fertile, well-irrigated and intelligently planted farmland moved him and he was able to trace and admire the fact that the variety of plantings reflected the changed nature of the soil as they approached the acid lava of the old volcanos he saw on the horizon.

He wondered what questions he might ask the oracle. His business prospered, he loved his wife and his children, his investments were insured and his health was splendid. He couldn't think of anything to ask her. He had been told by his American friend that she was a terrifying presence, so frightening that it was sometimes difficult to ask her your prepared questions. He tried to imagine some traditional monster with a head covered with adders and a mouth filled with fire, but he was either too tired or too drunk or too solaced by the beauty of the farmland to feel anxious about his interview with Gallia. His interpreter was telling him about her beginnings. The story was nearly as familiar as the radio music. Her family had lost the houses and villas that most families have lost at one time or another.

They arrived at the foot of the volcano a little before dark. "Aren't you frightened?" the interpreter asked. "Oh yes, yes," said Sears politely. He did not feel that he was giving the interview its importance. There was a little garden at the entrance to the prophetess's cave and Sears noticed that the soil was so acid it supported almost nothing but parsley. "Please let me take your arm," said the interpreter. "I'm so frightened I can hardly speak."

There was a sort of room in the cave lighted by a single electric bulb. Sears wondered where the power came from. The prophetess sat at a plain table covered with clean oilcloth. She was a middle-aged woman whose hair had begun to gray and who held her head high with her blinded eyes closed. She wore a clean cotton dress. Sears's feeling for her was one of absolute friendliness. This wonder, who had prophesied the fall of uranium prices, excited in him the broadest smile.

She asked to feel something of his and he gave her his wallet. She fingered the wallet and began to smile. Then she began to laugh. So did Sears. She returned the wallet to him and said something to his interpreter. "I have no idea what she means," said the interpreter, "but what she said was 'La grande poésie de la vie.'" The prophetess stood and so did Sears. They were both laughing. Then she held out her arms and he embraced her. They parted, laughing. Night had fallen and as soon as he started the car the chauffeur turned on the radio to very loud music and they returned to the capital.

This cheerful brush with a prophet was no help at all in Sears's understanding of Estelle. She thought her prophetic attributes of the first importance. She seemed to think of them more as an achievement than a gift. She felt that the world we see—the world Sears adored—was superficial and, in her case, transparent and that she could see a more real world where love and death were visibly ordained. It seemed to Sears that her foresight was largely pessimistic. She most often prophesied quarrels, poverty, divorce, madness and suicide. Sears could not remember her having prophesied any triumphs of the spirit. She dyed her hair red and wore lime-green dresses, and when you were introduced to her you would feel that you had met her at cocktail parties. I don't mean five or ten cocktail parties—I mean hundreds and hundreds of cocktail parties before that social ceremony vanished from the calendar and when the cocktail party seemed as much a part of nightfall as the lengthening shadows. She seemed so allied to the cocktail party that one wondered what would become of her when that ritual had become obsolete.

It would have been very unlike Sears to check on the accuracy of her prophecies. When they returned home in the evening after a party she would sit at her dressing table and say that it had been revealed to her that the A's would divorce, B would lose all of his money, C would be arrested for fraud and Mrs. E would go mad. She considered prophecy to be her outstanding social gift, and the complex irony of claiming to know the future was revealed one night to Sears when they were entertaining. Estelle was a dreadful cook—indeed she was a dangerous cook and she had that night prepared a risotto that was particularly lethal. While she prophesied lengthily the misfortunes of a family in the neighborhood, Sears worried a little about what he knew of the immediate future. He knew that at three or four in the morning that was to come every one of their twelve guests, poisoned by the risotto, would spend an hour or more on the toilet, racked by excruciating diarrhea. While Estelle, with her eyes half-closed, sketched the future, Sears wondered why her prescience should overlook that violence in the immediate future that he was able to predict.

Her ending was rather like this. She had been to a matinee in Philadelphia and had returned by train to the suburb where they then lived. She could reach the lot where her car was parked by an underpass beneath the tracks or by an unsafe wooden walk that predated the underpass. It was a winter dusk. She had started across the walk when a young man shouted: "Hey, lady, that ain't safe. A train is coming." "Who *do* you think you are speaking to?" she exclaimed, believing in introductions and other courtesies. "I happen to *know* the future." She stepped straight into the path of the Trenton Express and nothing was found of her but a scrap of veiling and a high-heeled shoe.

"Your male lover is a traditional invention of the neurotic," said Dr. Palmer. "You have invented some ghostly surrogate of a lost school friend or a male relation from your early youth."

"I'm not sure what you mean by ghost," said Sears. "It may be that for a man of my age love is rather elusive. I seem these days to know love only briefly, but I honestly can't agree with you when you say that Eduardo is a surrogate. He seems to offer me an understanding of modes of loneliness that are quite new to me and new I expect to other men, since they mostly involve new places like airports."

"Of course you're afraid of flying," said the alienist.

"I am not afraid of flying," said Sears, "but I am afraid of airports."

"Do you really think you understand Renée?"

"Oh, no," exclaimed Sears, "but I never really cared about those parts of her life that she meant to keep private. I mean, I kept picking her up in these church basements where she was trying to stop smoking or drinking or eating too much. Sometimes I thought it was all three. Sometimes when we go out to a restaurant she eats most of my dinner, but she never gets fat. I think she wants to improve her ways, and I believe there are more people who feel like this than you might guess from looking at the faces in the street."

"Do you have any friends?" asked Dr. Palmer.

"I have loads of friends," said Sears.

"That is," said the doctor, "the classical reply of the neurotic, who constructs a carapace of friendliness and popularity to conceal his clinical aloneness. If you have so many friends you might send a few my way as patients. The politics in this profession are absolutely indescribable. Otherwise I wouldn't ask your help. I'd like to see you tomorrow at the same time."

8

THE telephone was ringing when Sears returned to his apartment. It was Renée asking him over for a drink. He was delighted. Considering their last quarrel he expected her to be wearing the old blue wrapper when she opened the door, or perhaps nothing at all. He was smiling at this possibility when he entered the lobby and saw Eduardo, who laughed at the breadth of his smile. Here seemed to be a union from which jealousy had been leached. She opened the door as soon as he rang. He was disappointed to see she was not wearing the old blue wrapper. She was wearing a dress and some shoes and some perfume, but when she kissed him her kisses were of such an inestimable softness and variety that he didn't worry about her clothing. She gave him a drink and sat on his lap and unfastened both his shirt and his trousers. While she fingered his trunk he remembered that the gymnastics instructor at his school had lectured them on the fact that the male torso, disfigured as it was by vestigial nipples, was totally unresponsive sensually. He had, until very recently, never doubted this statement. This was really what one wanted, he thought. To have a lovely woman on one's lap as darkness fell from the wings of night was truly journey's end. She was kissing him when the telephone rang and she left his lap to answer it. "I'll be down in a few minutes," she said. "The doorman will let you double-park."

"What in hell was that?" said Sears.

"It was the man who's going to drive me to the airport." She went into the hallway, where he heard her open a closet.

"Where are you going?" Sears demanded. "You haven't told me you were going anywhere and you certainly haven't behaved as if you were taking a plane."

"You might have noticed that my suitcase is in the hallway. You always notice that sort of thing."

"I've noticed that your hallway is always full of suitcases," Sears shouted. "I've been stumbling over the damned things for months."

"Well, would you like to help me to the elevator with my suitcase," she asked, "or shall I ring for Eduardo?"

She stood in the doorway wearing a hat and a coat and pulling on her gloves. He felt himself approaching those bewildering spiritual mountains where he doubted the reality of his person and his world. He went into the hallway and picked up her bag. "Where in hell are you going?" he asked.

"I'm going back to Des Moines to see my daughter," she said. "I must have told you but you've forgotten." Eduardo, rather more like a custodial relative than a lover, regarded the suitcase, Sears's face white with rage and Renée's airs of a traveler with great composure. Sears's only commitment was to wait for her on the sidewalk until the car had its door opened and to accept her goodbye kiss. "You don't know the first thing about women," she said. He did not look back in the lobby at Eduardo and went to a movie. To scorn one's world is despicable, he thought, and he would merely observe that the theatre he chose was nearly empty, that the film was about werewolves and that a man in the row ahead of him had brought his dinner to the theatre and ate it during the film. When the movie ended Sears returned to Renée's house and found Eduardo in the lobby. He was pleased to see him as he would have been pleased to see a dear friend. "We've got to find something else we can do together," he said. "Do you like to fish? Would you like to go fishing?"

"Sure I'd like to go fishing," said Eduardo. "I've got some time coming, but I'll have to check with the union about a replacement."

"I know of a good bass pond upstate," said Sears. "There used to be a decent inn there. Do you have any tackle?"

"I think I have a couple of bait-casting rods," said Eduardo. "I'll have to look. My sons may have taken them."

"What do your sons do?" asked Sears.

"The youngest is a senior at Rutgers," said Eduardo. "The oldest plays jazz piano in a place in Aspen. That's in Colorado."

"Well, goodnight," said Sears. "We'll work out something."

"Goodnight."

Ten days later in a rented car Sears and Eduardo headed north for a pond near the Canadian wilderness that Sears recalled having fished ten years ago, although his memory was often mistaken and it might have been twenty years in the past or even longer. They left for the north on a rainy morning and this corresponded exactly to Sears's sense of the fitness of things. Eduardo drove until they stopped somewhere for lunch and Sears then said, "I'll drive." Eduardo tossed him the keys, and as soon as he started north in the rain Eduardo fell asleep. Sears was terribly happy.

He drove north on route 774, which had, like any main thoroughfare, changed greatly in the last ten years. Sears was not disenchanted but he did observe what there was to be seen. They traveled through what had been a neighborhood of small dairy farms, where the acre and half-acre fields had been divided by stone walls and light stands of timber. There were a few churches and farmhouses from the nineteenth century and even earlier that were completely unpretentious but that, in their charm and inventiveness, seemed outstandingly patrician. Seven seventy-four was now a length in that highway of merchandising that reaches across the continent. It would be absurd to regret the obsolescence of the small dairy farm, but the ruined villages were for Sears a melancholy spectacle, as if a truly adventurous people had made a wrong turning and stumbled into a gypsy culture. Here were the most fleeting commitments and the most massive household gods. Beside a porn drive-in movie were two furniture stores whose items needed the strength of two or three men to be moved. He thought it a landscape, a people—and he counted himself among them—who had lost the sense of a harvest.

While he drove he thought self-righteously of what he had done to improve the scene; what he had done for

Beasley's Pond. He had employed the environmentalist—Chisholm—and paid a laboratory at Cornell to specify the toxicity in the water. The reports were not completed, but there was to be a hearing in the town of Janice in the coming week. Chisholm spoke of the people who were destroying the pond as a huge and powerful criminal organization, who were bribing small municipalities and polluting water supplies to profit from the high cost of fill sites. Sears was not completely persuaded. Chisholm was one of those men whose worthwhileness, it seemed to Sears, was more of a genetic trait than a persuasion. One found them all over the world. The size of Chisholm's teeth, the thickness of his glasses, his stoop and the spring with which he walked all marked him, Sears thought, as a single-minded reformer. His marriage, Sears guessed, would have been unsuccessful and his children would have difficulty finding themselves. Sears was not far from wrong. Seven seventy-four seemed an extension of the destruction of Beasley's Pond.

It was late when they reached the inn. Sears was disappointed but not surprised to find his inn flanked by two fried-food shops. The inn had changed ownership many, many times since he had been there. They drank a lot at the bar but whenever they mentioned fishing the barman changed the subject. The kitchen was closed and they ate sandwiches for supper. In their room they watched a show on television and went together to bed. Sears woke up. He had no idea of the hour but it was that hour when one is given the illusion of insight. He went to the window. The fried-food places were closed but the window was open and the smell of fried food filled the room.

It was the smell of fried food that seemed to fill his consciousness. He thought, but only for a moment, of fried food as a new aberration like the strip with its cut-rate outlets and drive-in peep shows. He hastily amended this random thought with the knowledge that fried food had been one of the first things to be smelled on the planet. After the discovery of love, the importance of hunting and the constancy of the solar system came the smell of frying food. Even now, at the end of harvest in the most inaccessible of the Carpathians the shepherds come down from the mountains with their herds in the autumn to hear gypsy fiddlers and a snareless drum and smell sausages rotating over charcoal. It was barbarous—it disclaimed authority—and its magic was malnutrition, acne and grossness. It was indigestible and highly odorous and would be, if you were unlucky, the last thing you smelled on your way to the executioner's block. And it was portable. You had to be able to eat it as you sat in a saddle or rode on a Ferris wheel or walked the midways and alleys of some country fair. You had to be able to eat it with your fingers, picking it from a cornucopia of leaves or bark or human skin while you paddled your war canoe or marched into battle. They were eating fried food when they made the first human sacrifice. Eggplant was being fried in the Colosseum when they broke the philosopher on the wheel and fed the saints to the lions. They were eating fried food when they hung the witches, quartered the pretender and crucified the thieves. Public executions were our first celebrations and this was holiday food. It was also the food for lovers, gamblers, travelers and nomads. By celebrating and extolling fried food, all the great highways of the world kept alive our early memories of itinerant hunters and fishermen when we possessed no history and very little vision. It was the food for spiritual vagrants.

Eduardo was sleeping noisily when Sears returned to bed. Sears had been told that such lovers were always thieves, liars, felons, and sometimes murderers, but he thought he had never known anyone so honest. He felt then a surge of lewdness and with this some revelation that these caverns of his nature would never enjoy coherence. What he felt for Eduardo seemed more like nostalgia than the adventurousness of traditional love but it felt no less powerful. He saw then that if he was truly seeking purity he would never find it in himself.

In the morning they woke quite happily. Eduardo washed his hair with a shampoo that, Sears noticed, was advertised to make his head a glory of lustrous radiance. It reminded Sears of the happy and robust vanity of that time of life and—with no ruefulness at all—of the vast difference in their ages. How long it had been since Sears had ducked his head into a basin of water and combed his hair with the hope of appearing attractive.

After breakfast they rented an outboard. Fishing water was for Sears a creation with which he enjoyed a powerful rapport. He was enjoying this while tying a leader when the man who had rented them the boat came over and said: "I can't let you men go out without telling you that there hasn't been a fish here for about ten years. The last time the water was tested—that was three years ago, I think—it was a little more acid than commercial vinegar."

"Are there any other ponds around here?" Sears asked.

"Yeah, there're about a hundred ponds around here," the stranger said, "maybe two hundred, but they're all just as acid as this. Of course there's nothing to stop you from trying. The fish may be coming back."

They went out anyhow on the disqualified water and cast for an hour or so. Eduardo, Sears noticed, got his line out with commendable grace and expertise. When they brought the boat in Sears asked his friend what he was going to do with the rest of his ten days' vacation. "I'll take my wife to Key West," he said. "The union has package tours that you don't have to book in advance. I took her down the year before last and she loved it." They drove back down the strip again and it rained again. The younger man's company helped Sears to understand better the barbarity and nomadism of 774. They parted at Sears's apartment. "I'll see you when Renée gets back from Des Moines," said Sears. "Get a great tan."

9

AFTER the fracas in the supermarket Henry saw that Betsy needed a change. He got the day off and they decided to go to Chelmsford Beach. It wouldn't be as crowded as it always was on the weekends and they didn't much enjoy it with a big crowd. Betsy made a picnic, with lemonade for herself and beer for Henry, and they took off at about ten in the morning with little Randy and Baby Binxie in the carrier. It was a nice summer's day. They made the trip in less than two hours and they both enjoyed reaching the beach on a weekday when half the parking lots were closed and privacy on the beach was just something you walked into, which contrasted with their memories of the weekends when privacy was something you had to look for like a needle in a haystack. They found a nice place and put a parasol up over Binxie with his bottle. She and Henry had a nice swim and then she went up and lay on the sand and Henry gave Randy a swimming lesson. Henry kept shouting: "That's the way, that's the way, that's the way to do it!" He seemed very happy and excited. A little way down the beach was a group of very old people. They were so old that if they went swimming they would sink. They sat on the sand wearing all their clothes, including vests and hats, and one of the women kept saying, "Oh what have we done to deserve such a beautiful day!" Betsy didn't know what she was talking about.

Then Randy came running up and said that he had learned to swim and so she went down to the edge of the water and watched him demonstrate his stroke. She was very happy to see how pleased both he and his father were and she did not mention the fact that the buoyancy of salt water made it easier to swim in the ocean than to swim in the pools where she had done most of her swimming. Then they ate their sandwiches and Henry drank his beer and kissed Betsy and felt very amorous, but there wasn't any place and they knew that when they made love or even thought about it it made little Randy feel lonely and left out and they didn't want to spoil his day at the beach and she understood when Henry stopped kissing her. She had thought to pack a softball and Randy and Henry were happy to throw this back and forth, and she was happy to lie on the beach and hear the waves and smell the salt water.

Her people were not fishermen or sailors and she had nothing at all to do with the sea so far as she knew, but the brine and the blue sky and the sand all seemed most natural to her as if this were her home, although she could not imagine what it must be like to live near the sea with its winter storms and tempests. She had never in her life seen the ocean but on a summer's day. She went swimming again and again. Then the old people left and the shadows began to fall toward the sea. They packed up their own things. They were the last people on the beach and Baby Binxie was sleeping. While she gathered up the towels and the sandwich papers and Binxie's diapers she remembered watching on TV when an astronaut went into space. After the countdown the camera had shown all the people along the beach packing up their sandwich baskets and their towels and their folding furniture and going back to the parking lot, and she remembered that this had moved her more deeply than the thought of a man walking around on the moon. Almost everybody else on the beach had gone home early, and it seemed to her that they had gone because they had received some urgent message to leave and that the beach was their home and that on leaving the beach they would be like the evacuees of war or much more recently like those people who lived near toxic dumps and who have to travel for years, perhaps for a lifetime, seeking a new home.

"That was a nice day at the beach, darling," she said to Henry when they got to the parking lot and she kissed him. "I've always liked to spend a day at the beach and that was a very nice one." He kissed her and said, "I thought it was a very nice day too, but I'm going to ask you to drive until we get to route 224 if you don't mind. I'm sunburned and my eyes are strained and I'd like to rest before I hit the heavy traffic on route 224." "I know what you mean," she said, "but I'd love to drive." And so he got in the back seat with Randy and they put Binxie's carrier in the front seat and off they went.

"That sun made me feel poleaxed," Henry said and that was the last she heard from him. Then little Randy fell asleep and Binxie was already gone and she found herself alone in the car like the captain of a ship but a pleasant feeling of aloneness. She knew what Henry meant feeling poleaxed, but she had the strength to drive to 224 in a car with three sleeping and beloved men. Two twenty-four was a convergence of six- and eight-lane highways that made her think with longing of the simplicity of their day on the beach, when there was nothing more difficult to comprehend than blue sky and salt water. All the converging highways and the gathering whiplike noise of traffic made her wonder—foolishly, she well knew—if modern life with its emphasis on highways had not robbed men and women of some intrinsic beauty that the world possessed. She well knew that they couldn't have got to Chelmsford Beach if it hadn't been for the highways that seemed so alien. She was tired, very tired, and while she hated to wake up Henry she felt when they approached the intersection that it wouldn't have been safe for her to continue driving. There was a wide, safe shoulder a mile or two before the intersection and she pulled off onto this and said: "Wake up everybody. Your captain wants to go to sleep."

Little Randy didn't wake up at all and as soon as Henry took the wheel Betsy fell asleep and slept until Henry woke her when they got back to Janice. "I don't ever remember the sun making me feel so sleepy," Henry said. "Maybe it has something to do with the solstice. I feel like going to bed."

"Me too," said Betsy. "Did you take Binxie into the house?"

"I didn't do anything with little Binxie," said Henry. Then he shouted: "Dear Jesus Christ, I must have left him on the road shoulder up by 224. I took him out of the car when we changed places and I must have left him there!"

She hurled herself into his arms and said nothing.

Never had the importance of their love for one another seemed so clear. The cruel tragedy of the lost baby seemed endurable so long as they were in one another's arms. "You call the police," Henry said. "I'll go back to route 224. I'll have to go all the way to 427 to get it northbound."

"I don't know what to tell the police," Betsy said.

"Tell them we left a baby on the road shoulder of 336 near the junction of 224 northbound."

"What's the matter?" asked little Randy, who had just waked. "Why do you two look so funny?"

"We've lost little Binxie," said Henry.

"Is he dead?" asked little Randy with some concern and with some hopefulness.

"Of course not," said his mother gently. "But why don't you go in the house and see if there isn't something on TV." Then she kissed Henry and unlocked the door and went into the house with little Randy. She called the police and said: "I want to report a baby that was left on the road shoulder of route 336 about two miles before the junction of 224. The baby is in a blue bassinet."

"Is this a kidnaping?" the patrolman asked.

"Oh no, no, no," she said, "it was just stupidity, it was just stupidity."

"I'm afraid that's not our jurisdiction," said the patrolman. "You'll have to call the Department of Transportation." When she started to cry he gave her that number.

Horace Chisholm, the environmentalist, was driving southeast on route 336 late on the same afternoon. Chisholm had been, until a year ago, a high school teacher of bio-chemistry but he had come to feel that the hazards to the environment around him summoned him imperatively to do what he could to correct this threat to life on the planet or at least to inform the potential victims. He was returning from a town planning board meeting, where a zoning change would involve paving a half square mile for a shopping center while poisoning and corrupting some wetlands that fed two brooks that in turn fed sources of drinking water. That it would take ten or maybe fifteen years before the damage was seriously felt by the community had been the deciding fact in the voting. The feeling clearly had been that they would all be living somewhere else when the drinking water became lethal.

This turn of thought troubled Chisholm. The diminished responsibilities of our society—its wanderings, its dependence on acceleration, its parasitic nature—deeply troubled him. He could see it all on route 336. That a hermetic society had comparable limitations had never been called to his attention. He was a truly honest and conscientious man, but his wife had found him immobile and had left him. In fact she had obliged him to leave her and she and their two daughters were living in the house in Queens while he was living alone in a small apartment in the city. It was he who had been ousted but it was she who made the spiritual departure.

Route 336 was a deadbeat to drive for anyone, but for an environmentalist who had just lost some wetlands it was perhaps worse. The vote for the shopping center had been determined first by a promise of reduced taxes and then by pure irresponsibility. Any display of venality is depressing. Chisholm felt quite lost. Nothing waited for him in his apartment. There was no woman, no man, no dog, no cat, and his answering tape would likely be empty and the neighborhood where he lived had become so anonymous and transient that there were no waiters or shopkeepers or bartenders who would greet him. He turned on the radio but all the music he seemed able to get was disco music, and disco music from those discos that had been closed the year before the year before last for drug pushing or nonpayment of income tax. He seemed to be searching for the memory of some place, some evidence of the fact that he had once been able to put himself into a supremely creative touch with his world and his kind. He longed for this as if it were some country which he had been forced to leave.

He passed a blue car and was passed by a red car. Then he passed two light-gray cars and one brown van. He had gas on the stomach and a slight erection. He felt so lonely that when the car ahead of him signaled for an exit he felt as if he had been touched tenderly on the shoulder by some stranger in some place like a crowded airport, and he wanted to put on his parking lights or signal back in some way as strangers who are traveling sometimes touch one another although they will never, ever meet again. In a lonely fantasy of nomadism he imagined a world where men and women communicated with one another mostly by signal lights and where he proposed marriage to some stranger because she turned on her parking lights an hour before dusk, disclosing a supple and romantic nature.

He passed a blue car and was passed by two black cars,

a brown van and a convertible. His physical reality and the reality of the car he was driving were unassailable, but his spiritual reality seemed to be vanishing in a way that he had never before experienced. He even seemed to have lost the power to regret his past and its adventures. A pair of lovers in a car ahead of him—the girl was sticking her tongue into the driver's ear—failed even to arouse his jealousy. He seemed about to become a cipher. The pain, perhaps the most galling he had ever known, lacked any of the attributes of pain, any of its traditional bloodiness.

Then he seemed lost. He was lost. He had lost his crown, his kingdom, his heirs and armies, his court, his harem, his queen and his fleet. He had, of course, never possessed any of these. He was not in any way emotionally dishonest and so why should he feel as if he had been cruelly and physically stripped of what he had never claimed to possess? He seemed to have been hurled bodily from the sanctuary of some church, although he had never committed himself to anything that could be called serious prayer.

Then he saw blackberries in the scrub along the road shoulder. He could stop and eat some blackberries. That much would be real and true. His mother had liked to pick berries when they went for a drive. She had never forgotten the quiet lanes and roads of her youth and had never understood why her husband wouldn't stop on an expressway long enough for her to pick berries or violets. Chisholm was looking for blackberries, and blackberries that grew in a place where the road shoulder was commodious enough for him to stop safely and park his car. Then he saw the bright blue of the baby carrier. He didn't know what it was, but its brightness and blueness seemed to declare that it was worth his attention. It could have been some wrapping paper or a scarf or some other piece of clothing that had been thrown away by an ardent lover. There was no car behind him, and he pulled over onto the shoulder to see what the bright blue thing was. When he found a clean, happy baby waving its hands and feet he exclaimed: "You must be Moses, you must be King of the Jews."

Abandonment was the first thing that occurred to him, although it was hard to imagine such a clean and happy child having been abandoned. There might be a note, he thought, to explain the forsaken child, and he rooted around in the blankets but there was nothing but a half-empty bottle. The cleanliness of the baby's linen conveyed the fact that if the baby had been abandoned it had been a tragic abandonment—a cruelly enforced separation, a deprivation. He imagined a young, weeping mother. The sensible thing to do was to go on to the next exit and find a police station. The thought that the police might unfeelingly toss the baby into an orphanage aroused in him protective and paternal longings, although he was in no position to raise a child in his apartment.

He put the carrier into the front seat and, after waiting his turn, joined the stream of traffic. He felt himself distinguished. He felt his to be one of the few cars on the road that was transporting a pleasant baby. The next exit said GAS, FOOD and Chisholm took this. His first stop was a garage, where he got directions to find the police. They were in a municipal building from the twenties with an image of blindfolded justice above the door. Holding the bassinet with both hands, Horace had some difficulty opening the door. No one offered to help him. In the vestibule an arrow directed him to a desk where people, he supposed, brought their troubles, but seldom a smiling infant.

"I found this baby on route 336," he said, "a little before the turnoff for 224."

"You ain't shitting me, are you?" said the patrolman at the desk. "I been in the service thirty-seven years and no one ever told me they found a baby on route 336."

"Hey, Charlie," someone called from the back. "We got a call out for a lost baby if somebody found one. We got this broad in a place called Janice who said she forgot her baby on 336. We got a number to call. She's hysterical."

Chisholm was terribly happy. The baby went on cooing and gurgling and most of the staff of the station came around to look at him. To return an infant to its mother seemed to please everyone and it was decided that Chisholm should call her. "Mrs. Logan?" he asked when he heard Betsy's voice. "I'm Horace Chisholm and you don't know me but I found your baby on route 336. The baby is well and happy and waiting for you at the police station near exit 37." Betsy was hysterical, but when she collected herself she explained that Henry was on the road going south to pick up route 224 northbound and she gave them his license number. They agreed to call her as soon as Henry had been located, and the radio call for Henry hadn't been out for more than ten minutes when they picked him up. Then they called Betsy and waited around for Henry. The patrolmen had gotten possessive about the baby. "You can go now if you want," they said to Chisholm. "There's no point in your staying around. We'll give the baby to its father." "I'd like to see that the baby gets into the right hands," said Chisholm. To see the baby and his father reunited seemed to him some important part of the afternoon.

When Henry came rushing in and saw the baby in his blue bassinet he began to cry. He seized little Binxie in his arms and for the first time little Binxie began to cry. "I want to thank you," said Henry. "My wife and I want to thank you. We live in Janice and I wonder if you could have dinner with us tomorrow. My wife makes wonderful fettucini. That's green noodles. She makes them with spinach. We live in Janice, on Hitching Post Road. It's about an hour's drive from the city."

"I'd like to come for dinner," said Chisholm.

"We like to have dinner at around six," said Henry. "We like to eat early."

Late the next afternoon in his apartment Horace bathed and dressed, contented and secure in the memory of the fact that he had found a baby and restored it to its parents and would eat green noodles in their company that night. Continuity had seemed to be what he sought that afternoon when he had felt so painfully lost. Now he felt happy although he could not rig his hopes on the repetition of such an unlikely chain of events. He would settle for the evening. There wasn't much else he could do. It was the second time he had been to Janice and he knew the way. Hitching Post Road was not far from Beasley's Pond. When he rang the bell Henry let him in. "This is my wife, Betsy," he said. "I know you've talked with her on the telephone." Betsy looked at him shyly and said, "I don't know whether or not I should do this but I feel that I have to." Then she threw her arms around him and kissed him on the mouth. "Did you have any trouble finding the place?" asked Henry. "I've been to Janice before," said Horace. "One of the most difficult jobs I've ever had is Beasley's Pond. We're trying to clear up the pollution there."

"Mr. Salazzo who lives next door supervises the dumping," said Betsy.

"We'll have to cut the happy hour a little short," said Henry, "because Betsy doesn't like the fettucini to get overcooked. Her mother's Italian and in Italy she says cooking pasta is a regular art." They had some drinks and while Betsy was in the kitchen Henry passed a box of crackers that the label promised would stimulate conversation. There was no need for any of this, for their excitement at having reclaimed their son made their pleasure in Horace deep and spontaneous. The fettucini was good, and the fact that the light of the two candles on the table made it almost impossible for them to see one another made no difference to the pleasures of the evening. After dinner they settled down comfortably and watched their particularly favorite shows on television. At eleven o'clock when the entertainment ended Horace said goodbye and goodnight and Betsy shyly kissed him once again. It was agreed that he would call them when he next came out to Beasley's Pond. "We don't know how to thank you for saving Binxie's life," said Betsy. "Do whatever you can to save Beasley's Pond," said Horace.

10

THE hearing that Sears's enemies had rigged was held in the Janice town hall, a brick building from the last century. Considering the power and might of the organization Chisholm had described, the building seemed very modest. In the lobby there were posters urging passers-by to enroll in classes in karate, ballet dance and remedial reading. These aroused in Sears those taxpayers' blues that were so characteristic of his generation. There was an elevator with an OUT OF ORDER sign and he climbed a flight of uncommonly steep stairs to the hearing room. Breathing deeply—puffing—he became acutely aware of the fact that the air of the building was permeated with a disinfectant. It was pervasive and powerful and reminded him of the loneliness and regimentation of Eastern Europe, where even the grand-luxe hotel lobbies—even the Kremlin Palace—smelled of disinfectant. He was reminded again of Eastern Europe when he reached the upstairs hallway. Everybody seemed to be smoking and the hallway, filled with tobacco smoke, seemed like a glimpse at the past. How long it had been since he had seen so much cigarette smoke! He went on into the hearing room, where perhaps fifty people had already gathered. Some of them looked to Sears as if they had come in to get out of the rain that was falling and because they were welcome nowhere else. Chisholm was at the back of the room, engaged in conversation with a young woman, and Sears waved to him and sat in one of the front rows.

The room was a little like an informal courtroom, with a raised table for the authorities. They were not yet seated but there were name signs at their places. If the power of their organization was rooted, as Chisholm claimed, in Eastern or Southern Europe, you could not tell this by their nomenclature. Their names were so conspicuously up-country that they would have served — Sears thought — for third basemen in minor-league baseball. They seemed names from that rural past when one shared one's family name with backroads, lakes, bogs and sometimes mountains. The mayor, who according to Chisholm was a puppet of the opposition, was named Chauncey Upjohn and his lieutenants were named Copley Townsend and Harrison Porter. On the walls of the room hung two large photographs of bearded elders. Then there was a large photograph of the village after the catastrophic fire of 1832. Nothing had been left standing but chimneys. Also on the wall was a sculptured copy of the town seal. This was a portrait of one of the Nock-Sink Indians who had settled the river banks. The brave had a hook nose, a headdress of game-bird feathers and was holding a tomahawk with which, considering the bloody history of his people, he might have mutilated a Jesuit. Chisholm joined Sears a few minutes before the meeting was called to order. The two men had spent the afternoon in the wetlands around Beasley's Pond.

They had made the trip in waders. As they struggled through the marsh Chisholm recited a litany of the poisons the laboratory had promised to find in the water. In the water of the pond Sears saw islands of what appeared to be fermenting excrement. Where the water was clear one saw trails of vileness like the paraphernalia of witchcraft. "Pollution has brought in the rat-tailed maggot," said Chisholm. "Two years ago you wouldn't have found *Helobdella stagnalis* in a pond like this. Another newcomer is the sludge worm. Tubifex. *Glossifonia complanata* is also new." The only things that cheered him were the cattails (*Typha latifolia*) and *Phragmites communis*—the reed.

The wetlands drained into a stream that had for Sears the appearance of a traditional trout brook. It flowed over stones—glacial rubble—it formed deep pools, its breadth was variable, one could not quite anticipate its variety as it followed gravity through the woods to some destination of its own. The illusion of eternal purity the stream possessed, its music and the greenery of its banks, reminded Sears of pictures he had seen of paradise. The sacred grove was no legitimate part of his thinking, but the whiteness of falling water, the variety of its sounds, the serenity of the pools he saw corresponded to a memory as deep as any he possessed. He had on his knees in countless cavernous and ill-ventilated Episcopal churches praised the beginning of things. He had heard this described in Revelation as a sea of crystal and living creatures filled with eyes, but it seemed that he had never believed it to be anything but a fountainhead.

On and on went Chisholm's recitation of poisons. Polychlorinated biphenyls. Dioxin. Chloroform. Thoroviven. Clorestemy, Mustin and Thraxon. As they moved from the wetlands to the charming brook he recited the diseases these chemicals produced in men. Rickets. Blindness. Brain tumor. Impotence. Sterility. And these were all more desirable than what happened to the woman in Mitcheville who miscarried a child that looked more like a dog than a human.

Now and then the voice of the brook was louder than Chisholm's voice. A trout stream in a forest, a traverse of potable water, seemed for Sears to be the bridge that spans the mysterious abyss between our spiritual and our carnal selves. How contemptible this made his panic about his own contamination. When he was young, brooks had seemed to speak to him in the tongues of men and angels. Now that he was an old man who spoke five or six languages—all of them poorly—the sound of water seemed to be the language of his nativity, some tongue he had spoken before his birth. Soft and loud, high and low, the sound of water reminded him of eavesdropping in some other room than where the party was.

He remembered other voices he had overheard. One was at the end of some war in which he had been a soldier and was spending a day or two waiting reassignment or transportation, in a furnished room in some city where he was a stranger. He had been unable to sleep and had gone to the window to hear the strange city and had heard, instead, the voice of a woman from some nearby window. The voice was quite clear, weak with suffering and very appealing. "I don't feel like myself anymore, Charlie," the woman said. "I don't feel like myself anymore." The second voice that he remembered was very different. He had been a guest in a palace in Rome and had taken a bath in a room with a terrace. He had stepped out onto the terrace with a

towel to dry himself and to see the view. It was a truly
Roman view with clouds of swallows in the twilight and
grass, weeds and flowers growing vigorously from every
crack and orifice in the roofs and church spires that he saw.
Then across the roofs he heard a man shouting. "I will not
put my prick in your martini," he said and slammed a door.
Sears then heard the laughter of a woman although whether
or not her laughter was felicitous or bitter he had never
decided. He felt like an eavesdropper that afternoon, hearing the voices of the brook.

"That's the mayor, the one in the gray suit," said
Chisholm. "He's the worst of the lot, although the others will
do anything he tells them to. What our enemies have is a
great deal of money. They were taking twelve and fourteen
thousand dollars a day out of Beasley's Pond until we got
the hold order, and that expires at midnight." Sears regarded
the mayor. He judged faces, it seemed, on their capacity to
contain light. It was lightlessness in a face—the absence
even of the promise of light—that reminded him unhappily
of man's inhumanity to man. It was not, of course, in his
power or his disposition to judge the faces of strangers, but
walking down the streets of any city in the world he sought
in the faces of strangers the quality of light. Sears looked
for light in the faces of the mayor and his associates when
the meeting was called to order. There was an unfurled
American flag to the left of the table but the meeting did not
begin with a pledge of allegiance but with their singing "The
Star-Spangled Banner." The tape of an operatic soprano's
voice led them on. Sears had never before seen a thing like
this but then he had never before been to such a meeting.

Sears couldn't help noticing that the mayor was wearing a suit that looked expensive but was plainly a size too big. Had it been given to him by a friend? This seemed improbable since Sears felt sure he could have no friends. Sears also observed that the mayor was one of those liars who speak quite directly when they are truthful but who address their falsehoods to the fingernails of their left hands. It was a phenomenon that Sears had often noticed in bankers. "Beasley's Pond and the surrounding acreage," said the mayor, "were purchased a year and a half ago and declared a dump by the town planning board, with the approval of the governor's blue-ribbon committee on hazardous wastes. It was purchased by the Veterans' Committee for"—this was addressed to his fingernails—"the sole purpose of building a monument to the forgotten dead. The site has been chosen carefully. We used the exacting criteria we use for all hazardous-waste facilities. The population density is desirable. There is a suitable body of water. The soil is tight with good bedrock." Then he raised his left hand a little crooked, and said to his fingernails: "Exhaustive laboratory tests have proved that toxicity is no danger."

"May I ask to be recognized," said Chisholm, standing. "I have no objections to this meeting or to what you've said but may I propose a delay until our laboratory test results have been received?"

"Not until I've finished," said the mayor. "This meeting has been called," he said, "simply as a courtesy to placate a Communist-inspired conservationist, whose bread is buttered by an old man. Beasley's Pond is like the mainstream of American thought. It accords with human nature. To inter-

fere in our improvements on Beasley's Pond is to interfere
in the fruitful union between the energies of mankind and
the energies of the planet. To try and regulate with government interference the spontaneity of this union will sap its
natural energy and put it at the paralyzing mercy of a
costly bureaucracy financed by the taxpayer. Our improvements to Beasley's Pond are a very good example of that
free enterprise that distinguishes the economy and indeed
the character of this great nation."

"The plans for the evacuation of Janice are known to us
all," said a man who had not asked to be recognized but
who stood and read from a paper. He was a tall man with
gray hair and a face that, to Sears's taste, seemed inter-
mittently lighted.

"I have described this meeting as a courtesy," said the
mayor. "We have nothing to do with the evacuation plans."

"The urgency of the evacuation plans," said the stranger,
"is a day-to-day matter but I only want to bring up the fal-
lacy of a single point. As taxpayers we've been charged for
these evacuation plans and as taxpayers gathered here
together tonight we are entitled to discuss them."

"This has nothing to do with Beasley's Pond."

"The possibility of detonative contaminants in the water
has been admitted by your commission on hazardous wastes,
and since this would put Janice into a danger area with a B
classification it most definitely concerns Beasley's Pond.
But as I say my concern is over only one category in the
plans. The Chamber of Commerce, the League of Women
Voters and the Concerned Citizens of Janice have all
expressed their objections to the abandonment of the

imprisoned and the disabled and the general ignorance the evacuation plans display of the topography of Janice, its dead-end streets, inflammable buildings and high bluffs. All of this is on record. What I am here to protest is paragraph F in clause 18. This paragraph strictly forbids any congregating excepting at designated evacuation points upon designated summons. The idea here is that if a carcinogenic element is discharged into the air there will be fewer casualties if the population remains scattered. You are familiar with this clause?"

"Of course," said the mayor. He seemed defensive. "Of course."

"Under the best of circumstances the evacuation plans admit that no more than twenty percent of the population can be rescued. It seems to me that since so many of us must die we ought to be allowed to gather together in some house of worship and pray for life in the world to come."

"Who are you?" asked the mayor.

"I'm minister of the First Unitarian Church on Route 328. I speak for several other clergymen in the neighborhood."

"Do you realize," asked the mayor forcefully, "that the people of this great nation spend fourteen times as much money on breakfast food as they do in church contributions? The marketability of the church was exploded nearly six years ago when one of you clergymen endorsed a decaffeinated coffee and the firm went bankrupt in eight months. I can give you many more examples of how little of our national income goes into church contributions — pornographic appliances, for example — but I will confine myself to the fact that we spend fourteen times as much on breakfast food as we do in church contributions."

The churchman sat down. He seemed to be crying. Chisholm asked again to be recognized.

"I haven't finished," said the mayor. "I've described this meeting as a courtesy and I've encountered nothing but troublemakers. You, Mr. Chisholm, have, I happen to know, never served in the armed forces of your great country and you have no understanding, of course, of our wish to raise a memorial to our patriotic dead. You would like, I know, to prove that our fill in Beasley's Pond is comprised of leachates and contaminants. My father was an honest Yankee fisherman. He was a soldier. He was a patriot. He was a churchgoer. He was the husband of a contented, loving and happy wife and the father of seven healthy and successful children. If I spoke to him about leachates and contaminants he would tell me to speak English. 'This is the United States of America, my son,' he would say, 'and I want you to speak English.' 'Leachates' and 'contaminants' sound like a foreign language, and to bring governmental interference into our improvements of Beasley's Pond is like the work of a foreign government."

"I would like to request a postponement," Chisholm said, as politely as possible. "The Marston Laboratories are working on the specimens we gave them and they've promised a report by Thursday."

While Chisholm spoke the mayor conferred with the three members of the board and when Chisholm had finished he said, "Your request has been refused by a majority of the board, but before we close I would like to read a letter I have in my possession. This letter was written by your employer, Mr. Lemuel Sears, on the twenty-ninth of February last year and was published in the newspaper the following day. 'Is Nothing Sacred' was the heading of Mr. Sears's observations.

" 'I have been skating on weekends on Beasley's Pond,' he wrote, 'in the company of perhaps fifty men and women of all ages and for all I know all walks of life, who seemed to find themselves greatly refreshed for the complexities and problems of the modern world by a few hours spent happily on ice skates. The findings of the discredited paleontologist Gardener who claimed that the skate — or shate — was the turning point in the contest for supremacy between *Homo sapiens* and primordial man have been proven fraudulent — but isn't it true that we enjoy on ice skates a sense of fleetness that seems to be a primordial memory? Last Sunday, carrying my skates to the pond, I found that it had been rezoned as fill and had become a heap of rubbish, topped by a dead dog. There is little enough of innocence in the world but let us protect the innocence of ice skating.' That is your letter, isn't it, Mr. Sears?"

"Yes," said Sears.

"On one hand we have the grief of mature and thinking men and women who hope to commemorate the sacrifice of life made by their beloved sons and husbands in the cause of freedom. On the other hand we have this. The meeting is adjourned."

Almost everyone in the room, including the minister, looked at Sears with contempt. "I had forgotten about the letter," he said to Chisholm. "I wish they had," said Chisholm. Betsy Logan joined them and Chisholm introduced her to

Sears. Her view of him was obviously prejudiced by the letter. "The town board may give us another hearing," said Chisholm, "if the laboratory reports are devastating. It is still too early to be hopeless. We can try the district attorney, although he'll refer us to the governor's commission and the governor's looking for campaign contributions." They were almost the last to leave the hall and go down the steep stairs. Betsy kissed Chisholm goodnight and started up the street. "I'll call you as soon as I hear from the laboratory," said Chisholm. They shook hands on the sidewalk, but as Chisholm started to cross the street a car that had been double-parked and was without lights came down the street at a high speed and struck Chisholm with an impact that killed him dead.

11

Some few hours later love music was playing at Buy Brite when Betsy chose a cart and pushed it past the fruits and vegetables that were the first things to be found on entering the place. It was well after midnight. The music was faint—too faint to be identified—but almost anyone would recognize it as a love song. The lingering ups and downs of the melody had never meant anything else. To the music of love Betsy pushed her cart through the vastness of a nearly empty market, although the place was flooded with light. She was sad and vengeful. Chisholm had saved the life of her son. She missed him painfully and felt that the world would miss this pure and helpful man. Her cart was empty and in her raincoat pocket she carried a bottle of Teriyaki Sauce to which she had added enough ant poison to kill a family. Pasted to this was a message that said: "Stop poisoning Beasley's Pond or I will poison the food in all 28 Buy Brites." She had made this of words cut from a newspaper while her sons and her husband slept.

Betsy headed for the aisle where spices and extracts were displayed. She couldn't clearly remember where she had found the Teriyaki Sauce on that rainy afternoon when she and Maria Salazzo had battled. She pushed her empty cart past the shelves of spices and extracts again and again.

The search for anything, she knew, could be deceptive. How often had she looked for labels, prices and trade names in what was truly a crossroads of her time. Whenever she couldn't find what she looked for she always seemed to hear a chorus of elderly women in her family asking for their eyeglasses, their door keys, and lamenting the loss of telephone numbers, addresses and names. Oh where was the Teriyaki Sauce? She was anxious at the thought that they might have discontinued it or exhausted their supply. That someone might seize her, find the sauce in her pocket and sentence her to jail for having threatened to poison the community was, of course, an absurd anxiety but it remained very keen.

She went from the aisle for spices and extracts to the aisle for sauces and condiments. She had forgotten there were so many. She felt hopeful when she saw some exotic sauces and then she remembered that there was an Oriental corner between the baked goods and the dairy products. Here were the bottles of Teriyaki Sauce, and she left her bottle of poison on its side where it would be noticed. She left the store without anyone having seen her face. She climbed into bed with Henry but she felt too excited to sleep. It seemed to be the fear of being apprehended that kept her awake; but she felt that her bottle and its message would be discovered in the morning. World press would print the story since our supermarkets are such an axial part of our way of life. The story would appear everywhere including Russia and the Orient and the dumping in Beasley's Pond would end at once.

Nothing of the sort happened. In the evening paper

the principal story was about an unidentified flying object, seen by the wife of the chief of police, and some vandalism at the high school. Why Betsy should continue this project when there was so much in her life that contented her is a mystery. Her love for Henry and the children was quite complete, it seemed happily to transcend her mortality, and yet beyond this lay some unrequited melancholy or ardor. She was one of those women whose nostalgia for a destiny, a calling, would outlast all sorts of satiation. It seemed incurable. The next day she bought and poisoned some sauce and while Henry slept she made another sign and returned to Buy Brite. Her first jar had vanished but she put her second on the shelf, bought a box of Flotilla and came home. "Where were you, my darling?" Henry asked when she returned to bed. "Oh my darling, where were you?" "I couldn't sleep," she said. "I've been reading."

In the evening paper there was still nothing but news of the customary gains and losses and the next day she poisoned a third bottle and took it to the store when Henry fell asleep. When she returned Henry was aroused and angry. "Where were you, where in hell were you? You weren't downstairs reading. I've looked for you everywhere." She calmed him — he was a most amiable man — and they returned to bed but in the next night's paper she saw that she had been successful. POISONED FAMILY IN SATISFACTORY CONDITION, was the headline. "The Grimaldo family, disabled by a jar of poisoned Teriyaki Sauce, were reported to be satisfactorily recovering in the Janice Hospital. Whoever poisoned the sauce threatened to poison food in all the Buy Brite super-

markets until the pollution of Beasley's Pond is ended."
This time the news went all the way around the world, and
the dumping in Beasley's Pond ended at once.

Sears's business associates respected his success but
those who knew him intimately—those who played bridge
with him, for example—thought him not terribly intelligent. However, he was trusted and as soon as he learned
that the dumping at Beasley's Pond had ended, he organized
the Beasley Foundation. This took hours of tiring work
with lawyers and was one of the most difficult projects he
had ever accomplished or—he liked to think—that he had
ever seen accomplished. The foundation was financed with
assets taken from the Cleveland branch of the Computer
Container Intrusion System. This subdivision then became
a holding company with the status of a tax shelter and
short-term bonds that enjoyed a triple-A rating.

Only a third of the pond had been filled, the despoiled
end was dredged and an innovative aeration system was
installed to cure the water of its toxicity. At the time of
which I'm writing most of our great rivers and bodies of
water were in serious danger, and when engineers from
other countries came to assess the system, Sears sometimes joined them as a guide. His grasp of the language
was rather like a tourist's grasp of another language. "After
the dumping had ended," he could be heard to say, "we
were faced with eutrophication. The end result of the
eutrophication process is the development of a swamp or
bog, which eventually dries into organic mulch, devoid of

water. Historically the eutrophication and decay of a lake required tens and thousands of years, but with the increase of man-made contaminants and leachates it can be accomplished in no time at all." Sears liked to think that the resurrection of Beasley's Pond had taught him some humility, but his humility was not very apparent. When a visiting engineer offered to help him across a stream he said: "No thank you. I'm wearing the same belt I wore when I played football in college."

The loveliness of the landscape had been restored. It was in no way distinguished, but it could, a century earlier, have served as a background for Eden or even the fields of Eleusis if you added some naked goddesses and satyrs. "Our first approach to the problem was to pump bottom water to the surface, where it could absorb oxygen," said Sears. "As well as poisons, the dumping had brought nutrient chemicals into the water. These increased the algae and weeds. We had anaerobic conditions in the bottom water since it was completely devoid of oxygen. Hydrogen sulfide was released and manganese, iron and phosphates were dissolved from the underlying soil. Organic acids were produced and the pH of the water decreased. This destroyed all crustacea and other animals and ended the pond's life cycle.

"Bringing bottom water to the surface," he went on, "had worked well in small impoundments but this required considerable amounts of power per unit volume. We needed a new approach. We needed increased horsepower efficiency — we needed to move ten to one thousand times as much water per horsepower as provided by old techniques. We needed to reduce the bubble-rise rate — if the bubble-rise rate could be reduced to less than one fps, turbulent flow would be eliminated and a laminar uplift effect would be created. We needed to reduce bubble size. If the air were introduced in tiny bubbles at bottom level not only would oxygen be dissolved quickly and laminar uplift produced, but strata turnover would be continuous and the cold water of the bottom layer would be distributed into the surface. This would prevent water-quality deterioration.

"Our engineers developed a small-diameter plastic pipe with tiny apertures in a straight line. This can be seen in the office. The piping made for easy installation, reasonable cost and small-bubble formation. We put down 4,500 feet of this valved polyethylene tubing. The permanence of this was made possible by embedding a continuous lead line in a thickened portion of the pipe wall, opposite the line of apertures. The diameter of the tubing is 0.5 inch. The apertures—which are die-formed check valves—were sized and spaced to meet water depths and desired circulation rates. The weight of the lead keel embedded in the tubing was heavier than the water despite the advanced stagnation in Beasley's Pond. We then connected this piping to nine three-quarter-horsepower compressors with nine thousand feet of weighted feeder tubing. Air delivered by blowers at 4.4 cfm 30 psi continuously mix and turn over upward of three hundred million gallons of water. We have two auxiliary blower units in case of mechanical trouble. Fish kill has been cut by two-thirds and last month we ran tests at four water levels. These showed water temperatures of eighty-four degrees and dissolved oxygen of seven to nine mgl at all levels. A year ago the water was poison.

Now it is quite potable." Sears spoke with an enthusiasm that sprang from the fact that he had found some sameness in the search for love and the search for potable water. The clearness of Beasley's Pond seemed to have scoured his consciousness of the belief that his own lewdness was a profound contamination.

The visitors drifted over to the office to see the compressors and the pipe diagrams. Sears walked around the edge of the pond to the beginnings of the brook. Some mint grew here and he broke a leaf in his fingers. It was in the early summer but the sun was hot. The sound of water and the broken leaf reminded him of waking one morning with Renée. It was early. It was the first of the light. She lay in his arms and smelled of last night's perfume and of her own mortality, her yesterday. Her eyelashes had been dyed black and these contrasted with her blondness. They seemed quite artificial. The beauty of her breasts was no longer the beauty of youth and he knew that she worried about their size. He thought this charming. Her hair was not long but it was long enough to need some restraint, and she had, the night before, pulled up her hair—he could easily imagine the gesture—and secured it with a gold buckle. He had not seen her do this but now he saw the gold buckle and the hair it contained and the strands that had escaped. He kissed the loveliness of her neck and caressed the smoothness of her back and seemed to lose himself in the utter delight of loving. It seemed, in his case, to involve some clumsiness, as if he carried a heavy trunk up a staircase with a turning.

The sky was clear that morning and there might still have been stars although he saw none. The thought of stars contributed to the power of his feeling. What moved him was a sense of those worlds around us, our knowledge however imperfect of their nature, our sense of their possessing some grain of our past and of our lives to come. It was that most powerful sense of our being alive on the planet. It was that most powerful sense of how singular, in the vastness of creation, is the richness of our opportunity. The sense of that hour was of an exquisite privilege, the great benefice of living here and renewing ourselves with love. What a paradise it seemed!

The Salazzos packed their charcoal broiler and their stand-up swimming pool and vanished. Betsy told no one but Henry that she had threatened to poison the community, and she did not tell Henry until some time later. But, you might ask, whatever became of the true criminals, the villains who had murdered a high-minded environmentalist and seduced, bribed and corrupted the custodians of municipal welfare? Not to prosecute these wretches might seem to incriminate oneself with the guilt of complicity by omission. But that is another tale, and as I said in the beginning, this is just a story meant to be read in bed in an old house on a rainy night.

John Cheever was born in Quincy, Massachusetts, in 1912, and went to school at Thayer Academy in South Braintree. He is the author of seven collections of stories and five novels. His first novel, *The Wapshot Chronicle*, won the 1958 National Book Award. In 1965 he received the Howells Medal for Fiction from the National Academy of Arts and Letters and in 1978 he won the National Book Critics Circle Award and the Pulitzer Prize. Shortly before his death in 1982 he was awarded the National Medal for Literature.